THE BOYS
OF
1960

R. J. BURROUGHS

TATE PUBLISHING
AND ENTERPRISES, LLC

Published by Tate Publishing & Enterprises, LLC
127 E. Trade Center Terrace | Mustang, Oklahoma 73064 USA
1.888.361.9473 | www.tatepublishing.com

Tate Publishing is committed to excellence in the publishing industry. The company reflects the philosophy established by the founders, based on Psalm 68:11,
"The Lord gave the word and great was the company of those who published it."

Published in the United States of America

ISBN: 978-1-68301-510-9
1. Fiction / Small Town & Rural
2. Fiction / Action & Adventure
16.04.06

1

Another summer was beginning. It was what the five boys lived for. It wasn't that they disliked school all that much, school just took up so much time. They had to beat the second bell each morning; beating the first was near impossible. The second bell rang at 7:45 a.m., and the last bell of the day rang at 3:30 p.m. That was almost eight hours of your their wasted. By the time they got out, took all their books home, got into fun pants—fun pants being jeans too worn to wear to school—it was near 4:30 p.m.

Most families, including Sonny's family, had supper around 5:30, which didn't leave much time to do anything before dark. At least, the boys didn't seem to get into all that much trouble during the months that school was in session. Sonny and his friends did get into some little skirmishes with one or more of their teachers. Charlie received five swats from the *Thing* for taking the little ringer out of the bell in the school hallway. The *Thing* is the paddle hanging in the principal's office.

Bruce received four swats for having a smutty mind. Mr. Kilker, his homeroom teacher, said he caught Bruce trying to look up Linda Woodson's dress. The other boys had a field day with that. There wasn't a day went by that one of them didn't ask Bruce what kind of skivvies Linda was wearing. "Just shut up. Shut the hell up. You know I didn't look up her dress. What the heck do I care what's under that stupid dress?" he would say to whichever one decided to tease him at any given time.

When one or all of them happened to walk by Linda, she would make a face that would, sure enough, scare the holy crap out of the devil himself. When she gave Sonny the look, he thought he could also tell she was doing her best to hold back a smile.

Just as the boys were finishing the eighth grade, Sonny received the school record for swats—fourteen all together. That record stood all the years the five boys attended Verden Public Schools. The practice of giving swats to students was done away with so that swat record will last forever. The weekend before school let out for the summer, the boys attended a movie called *Some Like it Hot*. They didn't care all that much for the movie. They were more into cowboy or war movies. They thought *Some Like It Hot* was going to be a thriller but it turned out to be a kissing-type movie. They left about halfway through it. They even tried to get their money back but the manager wouldn't agree that it had been false advertising. They had spent a whole $1.75 (thirty-five cents apiece) to get into that stupid movie.

The only person that got anything out of it was Sonny. When Marilyn Monroe showed up in a bra, it got Sonny to thinking. Right there in the middle of the theater, he decided he could unsnap a girl's bra using only his thumb and a finger. That is what got him the fourteen swats at school. Walking up behind Mary Sue Bailey, he could see the outline of her bra through her white blouse. Before anyone could stop him, he put his bra-unsnapping plan into action. He wasn't in his right mind at the time but telling that to the principal wouldn't have done any good. No, he reached up using only the two digits and *snap!* The bra popped open as slick as you please. Charlie was standing beside Sonny, watching it all take place. Sonny smiled as he turned to Charlie but when he saw the look on Charlie's face, the realization of what he just did came screaming home to him.

Mary Sue dropped her books on the very spot, holding her arms to cover herself. She turned to look into Sonny's eyes, and the look she had on her face was the look a person would get the instant they were struck by lightning. Fear, excitement, disgust, and pure wonderment were all wrapped up into one horrific stare. Her eyes were open so wide it was a wonder that the skin holding them in place didn't tear like a piece of paper.

If there had been a mousehole anywhere around, you can bet Sonny would have found a way to get his body into it. He also dropped his books while looking into Mary Sue's eyes. People around him said he turned as white as a sheet. It looked like he was starting to get weak in the knees. Most people thought he was about to pass smooth out. Luckily—or was it unlucky—Mr. Snow was standing just outside his classroom and saw everything that just happened. Before Sonny could pass out or slither into any mousehole, Mr. Snow snatched him up and half dragged, half carried him to the principal's office.

For several weeks after that, the teasing was no longer focused on Bruce, but on Snap. Yes, they nicknamed Sonny, Snap. Every time one of them called him Snap, his answer was always the same, "Good gosh almighty! What in God's name drove me to do that?" When he got home from school that afternoon, his mother was waiting for him. The boys weren't sure exactly what happened to him but Sonny wasn't seen at all the next weekend. Jake thought the boys should peek in one of Sonny's windows to see if his mother, or worse, his grandmother, might have committed homicide on him. When school started that Monday, Sonny just barely beat the last bell, no worse for wear. The boys all met at the playground after school to make plans for the summer. At fourteen, they still didn't do all that much planning. It never failed that if they planned too far ahead, something always came up to either change their plans or something would come up, then they would forget those plans all together. Sonny really wanted to do his best to stay out of trouble this summer—or at the very least, not do anything stupid enough that Grandmother might find out about.

His grandmother said he had a memory span that would make a chicken look smart. "Boy, I have me eleven chickens in the pen out back, and I swear to the good Lord that as dumb as those chickens are at times—let me change that, most of the time, any one of those birds are smarter than you are. Only thing I am sure of is, you will always make it to supper. The only reason behind that is your stomach has the decency to tell you it's time to eat." She brought those chickens up as examples more times than Sonny could count.

After the boys all sat around and talked for a few minutes Bruce, Jake, and Charlie decided they better get home to do some of the things their folks asked them to get done. They wanted meet that evening at the theater to watch a new movie called *Psycho*. Verden usually didn't get movies until they were at least a year or two old. Gary and Sonny decided to head to the grocery store. Gary had four cents and Sonny had six; together, that was enough to buy an RC Cola. They had no problem sharing a pop between one another. Perhaps that was because in 1960, people didn't know all that much about germs. To tell the truth, the boys really didn't care about stuff like that. They cared about a cold pop. Sharing a cold pop with one of your buddies had to be one of the best feelings a couple of guys could experience.

Walking past the small house just north of the Verden Bank, they saw Miss Panoske sitting on her front porch. As always, she had an empty coffee can in her lap that she used to spit into. Leaning against the wall next to her chair was a double-barreled shotgun. Sonny had asked his grandmother why when Miss Panoske sat on her porch, she always had that shotgun within arm's reach.

"The reason that old bitty has that gun is because of a stupid ink pen," she said while pouring him a glass of milk.

"An ink pen?" Sonny asked.

"One afternoon, Ms. Panoske went to the bank next door to her house to cash a check or something. Standing in line behind a couple of people, she happened to notice Ivona Watson pull the little pen away from the pen holder, breaking the little chain used to hold it in place," his grandmother said, placing the milk back in the icebox then sitting back down at the table.

She leaned closer to him as if there had been other people in the kitchen that might overhear what she was about to say. This made Sonny look around, wondering if someone might really just be there. "Boy," she said, getting his attention back on her and the story she was about to tell him about Miss Panoske, "seeing Ivona placing the pen in her purse, Ms. Panoske went to hollering so loud you would have thought one of them badgers or bobcats you hear most of the no-account men around town talking about going out and catching all the time had done took a heck of a bite out of her fat butt. A couple of people that were just walking into the bank hearing her screaming about the pen, just turned around and walked smoothly away. They must have thought an armed robbery was taking place and didn't want to get involved or worse, shot graveyard dead from a stray bullet."

She continued. "Miss Panoske's outburst startled the teller, Lucy Talkington, so much she pushed the panic button. Banks back in the '40s, the alarm buttons didn't connect to the sheriff's office like they do today. The button only connected to a horn inside the bank as well as one outside just over the two doors. You can only imagine how loud things were with Ms. Panoske's screaming and the horns going off inside as well as the one outside," she said, smiling again and looking around. For only God himself would know who she thought might be there. Ivona went back, screaming that she didn't steal a pen. She said that Miss Panoske had to be doing some kind of hallucination. That or she was having one of them little clots in her brain that make a person see and do crazy things. Or worse, that she had to be one of them schizophrenia-type people. And if that was the case, she should be locked up before it overtook her mind completely, and she starts walking around Verden shooting the town folks plumb to death.

Ivona was screaming all of this, trying to get her voice heard over the screaming of Ms. Panoske and the two horns going off. Mr. Dobb, the assistant bank manager, came running out from the vault. He pushed or pulled a button shutting of the two horns, leaving the only sound of the two women trying to scream over one another. Mr. Dobb was a God-fearing man. If the doors were opened at his Pentecostal church, you could just about bet he would be setting somewhere inside. 'Ladies, ladies,' he said in a meek voice that wouldn't scare a thing. That didn't so much as get the two women screaming to even look his way. So then he screamed at the top of his lungs, 'Ladies! Ladies, would you please listen?' For some reason, that did the trick or maybe the two women had just worn themselves out from screaming at one another. 'What's the problem here? Whatever it is, I am sure it is just a misunderstanding. Something that can be settled between the two of you easy enough,' he said. 'Now, Ivona, can you please explain what the problem is between the two of you?' he asked her.

'"Why do you ask her to explain? She is the thief that has caused the problem to start with,' Ms. Panoske said, pointing first at Ivona's face then to the large black bag she had strapped over her shoulder. 'Okay, okay, then tell us what the problem is so we can come up with some kind of a solution,' Mr. Dobb said, looking from one to the other. 'It's like this Mr. Dobb. I was waiting in line to cash me a check for seven dollars because I found out old man Osborn was coming to town this afternoon to sell some cantaloupe and them burpless cucumbers. I just love his cantaloupes, not to mention the burpless cucumbers. A young woman my age can only eat the burpless ones, you know. Wouldn't do to burp in the face of a young fellow trying to court you now, would it?' she asked, looking around the bank at the people still half in shock at what they just witnessed. 'A young woman, my foot. Wouldn't surprise me one doggone bit if you didn't attend class with Jessie James, iffin' Jessie James was to have come from Verden, that is,' Ivona said, looking at her with an I'll-get-you look.

"'That's when I saw Ivona pull the pen from its little base, breaking the chain holding it in place. I have to admit it confused me. Not only did it confuse me, it near scared the pee-waddling soup out of me. It was the first time I have been this close to a bank robbery,' Ms. Panoske said. 'A bank robbery? A bank robbery, my foot! Woman, you're have either been hitting the cider a little heavy or you have gone nuts from drinking too much of your bathwater. And as far as them burpless cucumbers are concerned, you could eat nothing but lilacs and no man would ever want to come within a hundred yards of you—at least, no man that has him a set of standards, that is,' Ivona said, starting to raise her voice just a bit. 'And why not? Why in the name of the good Lord, if I might ask, would a man not want to court someone like me?' Ms. Panoske asked. 'Let me see, I will try to be as civil as I can, Ms. Panoske. First, you are ugly. Your sister was also ugly. I never met your mother and father but by looking at you, they had to be ugly as well,' Ivona said, not smiling one little bit.

"If Mr. Dobb had not grabbed hold of the back of Ms. Panoske blue dress, there would have been one heck of a fight between the two of them right in the middle of the lobby.

"'As for a bank robbery, you have to have yourself a gun and take the money before it is a bank robbery, you old poop you,' Ivona said. 'Well, if it wasn't a bank robbery, then it was a burglary—and a first degree burglary at that with all these people in here,' she answered. 'And, ugly, am I? I'll show you ugly. I'll show you what ugly really is when I find you alone one day. I'll tear into you like there is no tomorrow. And my name-calling friend, there just might not be a tomorrow for you after I finish with you,' Ms. Panoske said, with a look that could kill in her eyes.

"That is why whenever you see Ms. Panoske, she has that shotgun with her. I've been told she wraps a plastic bag around it and takes it in the shower with her, just in case Ivona sneaks into her house to waylay her in the shower after all the things she said to Ivona that day," Grandmother said, still looking around for some unknown person or persons.

Sonny had to hand it to his Grandmother. When she tells the story of one of the citizens of Verden, she tells it just like it was.

2

One afternoon, Charlie showed up at Sonny's home all excited about a conversation he had with Hobo Hobbs. Hobo Hobbs was what people around town called the town drunk. Some called him a just a plain old good-for-nothing hobo, among other names. His real name was Bobby Hobbs. They called him a hobo because most times, you could find him hanging around the railroad bridge a quarter of a mile or so west of town. Sonny asked his grandmother about him one evening while they were eating supper.

"Talk about a no-account soul. When you talking about Bobby or Hobo Hobbs, you're sure enough hitting the word 'no-account' right smack on the head with a big old hammer," she said, getting up to get a pitcher of ice water out of the icebox. "You know, no more than seven or eight years ago, he was a fine boy. Most anyone, or should I say everyone in Verden figured he would sure make something of himself one day. Heck, Old Man Franks down to the gas station once told me that it wouldn't surprise him one little bit if Bobby didn't end up as the President of the good old United States of America one day. Course, I never put much store in what Old Franks had to say 'cause I heard he did a lot of adultery around town. And you can never believe anything a guy that has been committing adultery might have to say 'cause they are sure enough liars. They have to lie to their wives as to their whereabouts so they can do their sick adultery," she said, sitting back down with a frown on her face.

When it came to Sonny's grandmother, she always had an opinion about everything.

"What caused him to start drinking like he does?" Sonny asked her.

"Well, hold your water, boy, I'm about to get there. Anyways, like I said before, a few years ago, we had us a barn-burning tornado come through here. It went just northeast of town. In fact, it came so close to Verden that there was just a gosh-awful lot of roofs got damaged. As close as it came, lucky no homes in town got blown away, just the roof damage was all. Anyway, Bobby was walking home when that thing dropped out of the sky. I was standing on that front porch right outside, watching that darn thing. Looked to me as if it was a mile wide.

Bobby apparently took shelter in the only place around as he headed home—that being the old abandon railroad bridge. I tell you, boy, it's a pure wonder Bobby himself didn't get sucked out from under that bridge and killed graveyard dead himself," she said.

"Anyways, when the storm passed over him, he climbed out from under that bridge and ran home as fast as his two legs would carry him. Once he got home—or where his home was supposed to be—there was nothing left. Maggie Sharp was the first person to arrive there right after Bobby. She told me there wasn't nothing left of the place other than the concrete slab the house was once set on. She said there were several dead chickens stuck in the remaining branches of the trees. Said that tree was stripped of most all its branches and all its leaves. Said it was about the funniest thing she had ever seen, dead chickens hanging where the leaves should have been. She thought she found a Chinese fellow stuck in a fifty-five gallon barrel up against one of them trees. However, when she inspected it a bit closer, she found it to be a scarecrow. I never found out why she thought it to be the body of a Chinese fellow.

"You know, boy, them tornados sure do some funny things," she said, smiling a little bit. "Come to find out Bobby's entire family got blown away. I'm told they found his pa in the Washita River about a mile away. His mother was found several hundred yards away in a plowed field. Poor thing was most covered with dirt. Only thing sticking out was the poor woman's nose, and one leg. To this day, his sister, Lillie, has never been found. Some folks think her body might have gotten itself blown all the way to the

Dakotas. The sheriff's office sent out one of the missing person's bulletins to several states but no one ever found Lillie. I figure someone just up and buried her, thinking they were doing a good deed and not knowing she had folks looking for her. Or she got herself hit in the head by a tree limb or board. Heck, even one of them chickens got blown everywhere. In that case, she may be wandering around, trying her best to figure out who she is," she said, picking up a few things off the dinner table and leaving the room.

"What you and Hobo talk about?" Sonny asked, getting back to Charlie.

"Well, he was telling me about a construction company that is setting off dynamite charges around the area. Apparently, when the dynamite goes off, they have a meter that will tell them if there is oil in the area. Hobo Bob said he found one of them little metal buildings where they store the dynamite. He said he took a box of dynamite, several blasting caps, primer cord, and a small roll of fuse," Charlie said.

"What did he want with all that stuff?" Sonny asked.

"Beats me. I guess he wanted to blow up something, Sonny," he answered, looking around as if he was expecting someone to walk up on them. When Charlie or one of the other guys looked around like Charlie was now doing, it only meant one thing: they were up to something. Better put, up to something that was about to get one or all of them in trouble.

"What have you done?" Sonny asked, looking around himself as Charlie's suspicions were starting to rub off on him.

"Well, Hobo needed a drink. You know how he shakes like a bird dog using the bathroom on a chainsaw when he is coming off alcohol. Well, he was out of money so I took my dad's bottle of bourbon and traded it to Bob for the dynamite," Charlie answered.

"My Lord, what are you going to do with dynamite?" Sonny asked, really looking around now.

"I figured we might sell it. I bet we could make enough money that we could all go to the carnival every day it's open this summer," he answered.

"Yes, we might do that or we might also get put in federal prison for the rest of our lives. First of all, don't you know it's stealing? Second, its stealing explosives, which falls under the FBI," Sonny explained.

"The FBI? I'm a goner. Don't they have a motto, something like, 'We always get our man'?" he asked.

"That's the Royal Canadian Mounties. Don't you watch *Sergeant Preston of the Yukon?*" Sonny asked.

"Ho, that's right. The Canadians always get their man," he answered, trying to smile.

"I don't think they are hunting you yet but they soon will be. As soon as that construction company reports someone stole the stuff," Sonny answered.

"Let's take it back, and then they will never know the difference," Charlie said.

"But what if they have already found out it's been taken? There might be FBI guys hanging out in the bushes, waiting for the culprits to return to the scene of the crime," Sonny answered.

"Sure enough. Good thinking. I've heard the crooks always do that," Charlie answered, looking behind his back again.

"Go get the stuff. I'll go get the other guys. Meet us down by the river near the Jenkins' junkyard," Sonny told him.

"Deal," Charlie answered.

Deal was what the boys used instead of *okay* whenever they were excited about something.

Gary, Bruce, Jake, and Sonny reached the stretch of the Washita River that ran just across from Jenkins' junkyard. The junkyard was so close to the river that a few of his old junks were only a few yards from the water. It seemed to the three boys that they had been waiting on Charlie for hours before he finally showed up carrying an old army duffel bag. He had mixed the dynamite in with what looked like several of his family's dirty clothes.

"I don't know all that much about dynamite. I sure didn't want it to jiggle together and blow me all over the county with people only being able to find pieces of me in the trees, like them chickens your grandmother told me about," Charlie said as he set the duffel bag down.

"Well, if that happens, it would sure save your folks a lot of money," Bruce said, smiling.

"And just how's that?" Charlie asked.

"Well, look at this from the eyes of an undertaker. First, if it was to blow up while you—well us—while we are this close to it, it would blow us into small pieces. I figure about the size of them little candy kisses. You know, the ones wrapped in the foil with that small piece of paper you pull to open them up? It would blow pieces all over. Most likely, birds, gophers, and all types of critters would then eat the pieces. No one would have a clue what happened. Only evidence would be a big hole in the ground where you were standing when it exploded," Bruce answered, smiling.

"That's right, but there is a silver lining to that, however," Jake said.

"Don't know how there could be a silver lining to that," Gary said.

"It's like this. After the birds or whatever ate the pieces, they would have to use the bathroom sometime. When that happens, you would be able to fertilize the land, helping things grow. It would be like you gave your life to feed the masses," Jake said, slapping Charlie on the back, causing each one the boys to laugh.

"Well, now what?" Bruce asked.

"We have to get rid of the dynamite Charlie got from Hobo Bob. If the police find out he has it, they will put Charlie in jail. He will be in so much trouble," Sonny said to the others.

"How can we get rid of the stuff?" Jake asked.

"Can't we just put the stuff in the river and let it float away?" Bruce asked.

"What if someone downriver finds it or what if it hits some bridge somewhere as it floats along and goes off? Might blow that bridge to smithereens," Jake said.

"Let's just blow it up. We got everything we need to do it with," Bruce said with a big smile on his face.

It only took Sonny and the others a second to agree to that. Blowing it up was the sure enough thing to do. Might not be the smartest thing to do but when you have a box of dynamite with the other things needed to set it off mixed with five fourteen-year-old boys, that had to be the only answer.

Charlie explained to the others what Hobo Bob had told him about blowing it up. "Hobo Bob said a fellow just had to stick one blasting cap into one stick of dynamite, wrap all the primer cord around all the rest of the stuff, tie the loose end of the primer cord around the cap, then stick the fuse in the cap, light it, and run."

"How long do we have to get away?" Gary asked with an I'm-not-real-sure-about-this-plan look on his face.

"Hobo Bob said one foot of fuse lasted one minute. So looking at what we have, I would say about five minutes," Charlie answered.

"We can't just let it set off on the ground?" Sonny said.

"Why don't we set it under that old car across the river?" Bruce asked, pointing toward and old 1944 Studebaker on the other side of the river. The front windshield was broken with holes in several places, the driver side door was gone, and the roof had been caved in. You could barely make out that it was once light-blue color with all the rust that had overtaken it, setting out in the weather all these years.

Setting off a box of dynamite in itself was enough to make the boys' mouths water but blowing an old car to smithereens was icing on the cake. The boys scrambled getting their clothes off to wade across the river. Once on the bank, the boys went about deciding where they would stick the dynamite to best blow up the car. This would have been a sight to behold if someone happened to walk up on five naked boys standing around an old Studebaker.

They decided one of them had better stand watch. It would be hard enough to explain to their parents them having dynamite, even harder to explain them having dynamite and naked. Bruce climbed up the far bank keeping out of site to make sure no one would walk up on them. Charlie pushed the dynamite under the driver's front door and shoved it to what he figured was about the middle of the car with a tree branch that Jake found. They figured once they lit the fuse, they would hide behind the large concrete block used to hold up the bridge a couple hundred yards down the river.

"I figure when this stuff goes off, it will blow this car into pieces about the size of softballs. The dynamite will be gone and the car will be gone with no one the wiser," Charlie said smiling, looking up at each boy.

They called Bruce back down while Charlie lit the fuse with a Zippo lighter he took off from his dad's nightstand. They didn't think the fuse was ever going to catch fire; seemed like all it was doing was melting.

"That's just our luck, a piece of worthless crap. I bet none of this stuff is real. Hobo Bob just needed a drink and conned Charlie out of his dad's booze," Jake said.

Just as the lighter was starting to burn Charlie's hand from being lit so long, the fuse began to hiss as it caught fire. The boys didn't stand around to watch the fuse burn. All five of them turned in a dead run and headed for the concrete under the bridge. Once behind the bridge, you could see nothing but five heads sticking out from behind the concrete. When the dynamite exploded, it went nothing like the boys thought it would. Instead of blowing the Studebaker into small pieces, it blew the car up into the air so high that the boys had time to come out of hiding to watch it hit its peak in the air and start back down.

"Good lord, it's going to hit the chicken coop," Bruce hollered out, pointing at the coop a couple hundred yards away from the junkyard office.

When the Studebaker hit the far half of the coop, all a person could see was red-and-white feathers flying around in the dust and several chickens running around as if they had just had their heads cut off. The shock of the car hitting the coop and ground so hard caused the old outhouse to explode as well, blowing the mixture from the hole all over the cars that were parked around the building. The boys tried to duck behind the bank but they were not quite fast enough. The crap that was in the hole hit each boy square in the face. Sonny had a piece of what they all thought was toilet paper hanging down from his head, covering his right eye. Several of the boys started to gag but getting back to the river seemed more important to them than throwing up at the time. Scrambling back into the river, they started washing themselves as they swam back across the river to their clothes. Sonny and Jake tossed up their lunch as they waded across. Walking back into Verden, the boys were surprised to see groups of people standing outside the stores, looking toward the river.

"What's wrong? What's everyone looking at?" Gary asked one of the men standing in front of the bank.

"Not sure, boy. People think there might have been a plane crash over by the river. Old Man Miller said he seen something drop out of the sky over that way," the man answered.

"I bet you it's one of them UFOs. Has to be. Didn't you here that big boom? That had to be when the UFO broke the sound barrier when it hit its brakes entering our atmosphere," some old man who was standing nearby said.

A couple of the men standing around him looked at him as if he had lost his old mind. "A UFO? Orville, you're plumb nuts, you know that? Heck, there aren't no UFOs anywhere's around here. All them UFOs hang out in places like New Mexico or Arizona. I believe it's because of the heat. It's a known fact that UFOs like hot weather," he said.

"Iffin' one of them little fellows has the know how to fly a ship all the way from one of them stars way the heck up there, then I reckon he knows how to put a heater in his spaceship," Old Man Miller said.

The boys wanted to tell them it was just them destroying a car, a chicken coop, and an outhouse. No plane crash or UFO at all. But if they told them that, they might as well tell them to go get the sheriff and FBI to lock them up as well. They all decided to let it well enough alone and went their separate ways until tomorrow. They figured the people from town would find out as soon as the owner of the junkyard came to town. He'd report someone blew up one of his old junk cars, killing half his chickens while destroying his chicken house completely, not to mention, all the crap spread over everything around the area.

3

The next afternoon, Sonny and Charlie were sharing a Coke in front of the drugstore when they overheard Mrs. Troop talking to Mr. Talking. They were discussing the old Studebaker being blown up as well as the two graves on Mrs. Troop's land.

Most people in town had figured out by then that the explosion was just a bunch of the older boys causing mischief. They thought it was kind of a rite of passage for boys go through before they become men. Still, there were a few that believed something else happened at that old junkyard. Some people were sure aliens were about to invade the town. Others thought gangsters had blown someone up in the Studebaker. In fact, five or six of the men from the pool hall were so sure it was gangsters that they went to the junkyard looking for body parts. Finding no body parts, they decided it had to be some of the older boys doing it as well. Seems there were always people that wanted to make something out of nothing; it was their way of adding some kind of spice to their lives. A few of the men in town looked like they really wanted to ask one of the five boys a question but since the boys were only fourteen, they changed their minds, thinking that they were too young to do anything like blowing that car up.

The subject changed to Sonny and Charlie's liking when Mrs. Troop asked Mr. Talking if he knew anything about the graves behind her house. She knew there were two graves in the backyard when she and her husband bought the house a couple years ago. She thought that the graves were far enough away from the house that they would never be in the way. Besides, the markers were surrounded by a small metal fence. However, since her children have gotten to middle school age, they were now playing in the backyard with friends. She was afraid they might get inside the fence and disrespect the two people buried there, if not completely destroy the markers.

Mr. Talking said he knew the two who were buried behind her house and knew what happened to them. He said the name on the first marker was Rick Sebourn; the girl buried next to him was Ernestine Grant. He went on to tell Mrs. Troop about what happened to the two. Apparently, they had been boyfriend and girlfriend from grade school to high school. They had a habit of going parking a few miles out of town every Friday and Saturday night if there wasn't anything showing at the Chief Drive-in just south of Chickasha. There just wasn't much for young people to do in Verden. Dragging up and down Main Street couldn't have been much fun either as that took all of fifteen seconds to drive from one end of town to the other.

You would have thought Charlie and Sonny were spies the way they were taking this all in as they moved closer to the couple, hoping not to miss a word. When people are talking about lovers, graves, young people, deaths, and killing all in the same breath, you can bet that completely grabs the attention of any fourteen-year-old boy within earshot.

Mr. Talking said the couple was to be married very soon; in fact, he thought they were to be married within five or six days of their deaths. Ever since Rick Sebourn was old enough to borrow his father's car and drive, they had been parking in the same spot. He figured that the couple apparently decided to do it one last time before their wedding. Anyways, Mr. Talking was driving by just about daylight that Sunday morning when he noticed the back end of Rick's '34 Ford coupe sticking out just a little bit from the tree line. If you knew Mr. Talking, then no one would have to explain why he went to check on the car. He knew as well as everyone else in Verden that the two kids were in love and about to me married. But if there was even a slight chance to catch them at something or other, something he could tell at the pool hall, then he wasn't about to miss that chance. You see, Mr. Talking was one of the biggest gossips in Verden, if not the biggest. Many a time he went out of his way to start a rumor around town or shared some sweet gossip about this or that person. Even if there was nothing to gossip about, he would come up with something, you could sure enough bet the whole farm on that. He was once overheard telling someone that gossip was about the easiest thing in the world to start. He said everyone—or just about everyone—loves a good gossip story; the juicer the better. He once started a rumor that Kayla Rich was going to have a baby. However, under his breath, he whispered that he was sure the baby she was having was part-Indian.

"I wonder how that happened?" he added, smiling that evil smile only he could conjure up. In less than twenty-four hours, the story about Kayla and her part-Indian baby was all over town. You could get different versions of the story according to whom you talked to.

Lucy Gorge said she was sure poor Kayla Rich had been hypnotized by some Indian medicine man. She said those medicine men are really into some weird stuff. The medicine man must have conjured up some kind of Indian magic using some Indian herbs and beads. She believed, but didn't know why for some reason, that Indians really liked beads. Anyway, using those herbs, shaking the beads, along with dancing around a campfire, must have been all the magic needed to make Kayla fall in love with some young Indian fellow. And that, she believed, is why Kayla is carrying an Indian baby. Another person thought something must have happened to Kayla in Anadarko, as she went there often. After all, wasn't it the Indian capital of the world? They figured it had to be something really bad, so bad, in fact, that Kayla wouldn't or couldn't tell another person about it, much less go to the sheriff.

The story finely came to an end one afternoon when Lucy Gorge whispered to Rachel Ashley in the store, "Did you hear about Kayla Rich? They say her baby is half-Indian."

Rachel answered, "No, I didn't know Kayla was having a baby. But I'm not surprised the baby is part-Indian because Kayla is half-Indian herself. And her husband is a little more than half himself."

If you had been standing beside Lucy when she heard what Rachel had to say, you would have thought someone pulled some plug out of her bottom, letting all the air out of her body. It hit her so hard she had to sit down by the display of cupcakes. You could hear her whispering under her breath, "I'll get even with you, Talking. I'll get even with you for this, you big gossip-starting liar."

Mr. Talking went on to explain to Mrs. Troop that something odd happened when he got out of his car to check on the couple. As he was walking up to the Ford, he felt a cold wind completely overtake his body. It wasn't a cool breeze by any means; it was a cold wind. He thought it could have been a force of some kind that surrounded him.

"Wouldn't you have been kind of nervous walking down to that car not knowing what you might find? Being nervous kind of makes a person sweat, you know. Then a cool breeze could have made you think it was cold," Mrs. Troop asked him, interrupting his train of thought.

"Nope, I know what I felt. You can believe me. It was a cold gust of air, just like I was walking down there in the middle of January or February. You remember how cold it gets then, how that north wind will cut right through a person. Well, that is sure enough just like what I felt come over my body," he answered her with what appeared to be an irritated look on his face.

Mrs. Troop kind of shuddered, thinking how strange that sounded. She was hoping this didn't turn out to be a horror story.

"When I got to the car, I bent over and looked through the front windshield. I saw Rick slumped over the stirring wheel. Ernestine was setting next to Rick with her head on his shoulder. I figured they must have both fallen asleep after several hours of smooching. Heck, I remember when my missus and I were young and did just some of that smooching ourselves. Kind of runs into work after awhile, you know. You have to keep adjusting yourself when this arm or that one falls asleep. It's work, I tell you," Mr. Talking said.

"Well, were they sleeping?" she asked, wanting him to get on with his story.

"Like I said, I thought they were both sleeping. I thought about knocking on the window to wake them up. I figured his or her folks must be starting to worry by then, but I thought what the heck, you are only young once. They was to be married real soon anyway so I just figured to let them sleep together. It would give them something to laugh about when they were an old married couple one day," he said.

You could tell Mrs. Troop was happy it turned out to be just a couple kids in love after all by the smile on her face.

"But then when I stepped to the side of the car, noticing the window was down, I decided to take one last look so I would have my information correct when I told the story around town," he said. "I looked in that open window and I near lost control of my bowels. Something I was sure glad didn't happen 'cause I ate me three eggs over easy, a short stack of flapjacks, two pieces of turkey bacon, and topped it all off with two pieces of gravy on toast, not to even mention, all the coffee I drank just that morning," he continued.

Mrs. Troop wasn't a violent person but if she happened to have a pistol in her purse about that time, she figured she would have pulled it out and shot Mr. Talking six or eight times for dragging this story out like he was. She figured no court in the land would convict her for it.

"When I looked in, I noticed that Ernestine's eyes were wide open. Not open like she just woke up saw me looking in at them, not by a long shot. Nope, her eyes were open like, well, open like someone just told her she was about to have a baby or open like someone done snuck up on her with one of them electric cattle prods and goosed her with the thing on high. I said, 'Hi Ernestine,' not knowing what to say to a young girl who has been smooching all night, kind of had me over the preferable barrel," he said, taking his ball cap off scratching the back of his head with his other hand. "But Ernestine never answered me back. I figured she must be embarrassed at me finding them like that. So I smiled and said, 'Well, I got to get myself home. I'm sure the missus must have breakfast ready by now.' Course, she had no clue all the food I had already eaten but it was all I could come up with in that short time. I sure didn't want to tell her I was just trying to get myself something juicy to talk about. But I'll be darn, when I started to walk away, I looked back at her, and you know what? Well, let me tell you. She hadn't moved one smidgen. Her eyes were staring at me just like they were when I was looking in at her through the window. I wasn't sure what was up with that girl. No matter which way I moved, her eyes seemed to follow me. The weird thing was they didn't seem to move on her face. It's like that picture of Jesus at church. No matter where you sit in church, those eyes seem to follow you. I first thought Jesus' eyes were following me because I tried to look up my Aunt Betty's dress when I was a young tike. You know Jesus frowns on that kind of thing but when you're a seven-year-old boy wondering what might be under that dress is a lot more important to you than the chance of burning in hellfire till the cows come home," he said.

Again Mrs. Troop wished she had that pistol or, at the very least, a knife or a large rock in her purse to either stick him or hit him. He was really dragging out the story of those two graves.

"Then talking about Jesus, it was like he come down from the heavens and just as hard as you please, slapped me smooth across the cheek when I realized them two kids was bad sick or worse, had gone on to be with the good Lord in the clouds above," he said, pointing to the sky. "Now let me tell you this, Mrs. Troop. I don't consider myself a coward by a long shot. Course, I am not the bravest fellow in town either. Only reason I didn't join up to fight them little Korean fellows during that war was because I figured it was a lot more brave for me to stay home and protect all the women and kids here in Verden. Heck, a fellow would never know when one of them Korean fellows might show up here in town and do all kinds of hurt to people. So I stayed right here, ready to face one or even more of them fellows if they happen to show up," Mr. Talking said, looking around in hopes someone else might be hearing what he was telling her.

Mrs. Troop started to look around. She didn't have a gun or knife but there were rocks aplenty. If he didn't get on with the story, she wanted to have one in sight to pick up and knock several knots on his head for wasting her time.

"There wasn't a thing I could do but go back to the car and reach in and shake them two kids, hoping Ernestine was one of them women you hear about who sleep with their eyes open. But when I grabbed her shoulder and shook her a little, her head slid off the boy's shoulder. I tried to grab her but I wasn't quick enough when her head hit that little round knob that turned the radio on. There I stood, looking at those two kids in that car with Johnny B. Goode playing loud enough to wake the dead. Course, I guess that isn't true because as loud as that music was playing, those kids didn't make a move," explained Mr. Talking. "Now don't get me wrong, I'm sure no doctor. Course, I did take me that first aid class down to where I work. But that sure weren't no help. All they taught me was how to put a bandage on a fellow iffin' he happens to cut himself. They tried to teach me that mouth-to-mouth thing you do to folks that has just gotten themselves a heart attack or one of them strokes like my aunt, Bessie May, did a couple of years ago. I was told she was standing in the supermarket talking to one of her Sunday school friends about canning green beans one minute, and the next thing, she was on the floor all sprawled out with boxes of Uncle Ben's rice all around her. They said she fell into the Uncle Ben's rice display as she was stroking out. She was plumb past mouth-to-mouth when she hit the floor. Them boxes of rice weren't much better, all smashed up and all. But let me tell you this, I'm not about to be putting my mouth on some man or woman who has drowned or had a heart attack. Who's to know where their mouth has been on? What if I was to give mouth-to-mouth to some fellow who had just eaten a big plate of liver and onions? Good Lord, I hate liver. The taste of liver on his breath might make me sick, and there we both would be. Besides, I'm not real sure if God himself wants a fellow to be bringing a person back to life once he has called them home. Nope, I'm not real sure if a fellow should be trying to second guess the Almighty," he said, looking around again. "When it's your time to stand there in front of the good Lord, you sure don't want him asking you why you gave so and so mouth-to-mouth and brought them back to life after he gave them that heart attack or done drowned them. Nope, I don't want that at all. So I'll not be putting no mouth-to-mouth on anyone, being the good Christian that I am," he said, looking her in the eyes not smiling a bit.

That was it for Mrs. Troop. She turned to walk away. She had all she could take of him. His story about this and that never got to the graves in her backyard. As slow as he was going, she figured if he ever did get around to answering her question, she would be ready for a grave herself.

"Anyways, I ran to the nearest phone and called the sheriff's office. Lord, I am here to tell you, not only did the sheriff himself show up, but a couple of highway patrol officers. It looked like we had Bonnie and Clyde cornered in the bushes. They took the bodies of them young kids to the coroner's office in Chickasha to let that doctor figure out the cause of death. Come to find out they was killed by exhaust fumes. Apparently, Rick had punched several holes in his muffler to make it sound like a hot rod car. I figure one of them glasspack mufflers was a little more than he wanted to spend, getting married and all. Apparently, there must have been a breeze blowing in on one of them or it might just have been an overly cool night. They had the windows rolled up tighter than old Mr. O'Dell down to the bank. Getting a loan from him for this or that is about as easy as slapping a bull on the butt and expecting him to turn around and smile at you. Anyway, while them two kids was a kissin' and a huggin', smooching and all, they must have left the car running, and the fumes came out of the holes Rick put in the muffler and up through cracks in the floorboards, taking the place of the oxygen in the car. I figured the kids must have been breathing heavy from the smooching that they thought it normal to be gasping for air the way they must have been doing. And before they knew they was in trouble, they got themselves killed. Before you ask me about the open window on Ernestine side of the car, I figured when she saw Rick turning blue— if people who get gassed turn blue, that is—she started to roll her window down. But by then, she had so much of them gasoline fumes in her own body that she just keeled over herself," he said, again looking around.

"Anyways, the death of them two kids, who grew up in this small town, hit Verden pretty hard. Heck, everyone in town knew them kids. The mayor wanted to shut down the town the day they was to be buried, wanted to call off school and close the bank. Most everyone in town was in agreement. They were going to buy that house you now live in once they was married so the town could bury them in their own little graveyard behind it," he said, finally.

"Well, what a sad story," Mrs. Troop answered. "That settles it for me. I will just have someone come look at the fence, strengthen it where it needs strengthening, and fix the gate. That should keep the kids from doing any damage to the graves. Mr. Talking, do you want to make a few extra dollars or do you know anyone around Verden who might want to be fixing that fence and gate around the two graves?" she asked him.

"I would love to make some extra money but I don't want to go anywhere around those graves, same as most people in this town," Mr. Talking answered.

"Why is that?" Mrs. Troop asked, a slight glimpse of a frown was starting at the corners of her mouth.

"Plain and simple, it's haunted," he answered.

When Sonny and Charlie heard the word *haunted*, their ears seemed to grow a couple of inches as they turned their heads to not miss anything that was about to be said. To two young boys, *haunted* is the same as *land ho* to a sailor who has been at sea for several months or *gold* to an old prospector who has spent his life looking for the elusive metal. Sonny elbowed Charlie and smiled at him, knowing an adventure was about to be bestowed on them from that one word.

"*Haunted*. I can't believe someone your age still believes in such nonsense as something being haunted," she answered him with an unmistakable frown on her face now.

"It might be nonsense to you or to a lot of people but for most of the folks here in town, it's not nonsense. It is a pure fact. Same as you shouldn't drink milk while eating chili 'cause it will make your innards just stop working for some reason. People from town believe this. I'm not talking about one or two, I'm talking most folks living here—well, who has lived here more than a year or two," he answered.

"What makes people think the graves are haunted?" she asked.

"More times than I can put my finger on, people have seen that young couple walking or sitting near them markers smooching, just like I figured they did the night they got gassed," he answered. "Just like when I told you I'm not a doctor, well, I'm sure no expert on the afterlife either. And let me add just a little footnote to that. I'm sure in no great hurry to find out about it," he said, turning to walk away.

Mrs. Troop wasn't real sure if Mr. Talking was a bit shy of knowledge. She sure didn't want to label anyone stupid but if someone was to hold a gun on her to make her come up with the name of a stupid person, Mr. Talking would be the first name off her lips.

"Well, if that don't take the cake out of the oven, I sure don't know what will," Charlie said to Sonny.

"I got a pretty good idea what's going through that head of yours, Charlie. You want to go up to the graves, see if that story the old man told was true or not," Sonny guessed. "Seems to me that after what we went through last summer, going to that hunted house should have cured us from ghost hunting." Sonny smiled at Charlie.

"Where's your sense of adventure?" Charlie asked Sonny.

4

The next day, Charlie and Sonny met the other guys in front of the theater. Sunday was the day the theater put new posters up for the coming attraction that week. When the usher, Larry Powers, opened the glass-covered case used to hold the posters, the boys started to jump around like they were watching the Sooners playing football and the team was about to win in the last few seconds of the game.

"I can't believe it. John Wayne. *The Alamo*. I don't know about the rest of you, but I plan on going in there and watching it over and over. Well, at least, until the usher tells me I have to leave. John Wayne, John Wayne showing in Verden. I can't believe it. I just can't believe it," Sonny said.

After they got over the excitement of *The Alamo* coming to the small theater in town, Sonny and Charlie started to explain to the others about the two graves behind Mrs. Troop's house.

"Who's for going up there tonight?" Charlie asked no one in particular, looking from one to the other.

They all agreed it might be a fun thing to do but you could see there wasn't a lot of enthusiasm as each boy nodded his head yes. They almost had the pee scared out of them last summer when they visited that house. Everyone said it was haunted. They didn't really see any ghost but that little thing with the window and curtain kind of put a damper on ghost hunting. So, a person couldn't really say anything about their lack of enthusiasm when it came to ghost hunting this summer. They all decided to meet at Bruce's house about thirty minutes before dark. That would give them time to walk to Mrs. Troop's house and find a good place to hide in the wooded area a few yards behind the house, which was only ten to fifteen feet behind the two graves. Walking to the Troop house, they all decided it would be best if they hid together. They were sure that if a ghost did happen to come out of one or both of the graves, strength was in numbers. Alone, a fellow would just about be dead meat; but as a group, nothing would happen or should happen.

As Jake put it, "Have any of you guys ever heard of a ghost confronting a group? Sure, you hear of people being scared plumb to death by a ghost, but have any of you ever heard of a group of guys been scared by a ghost?"

They all thought about it for a couple of seconds, and then one by one, each boy shook his head no. That little statement seemed to put more life into them. Knowing they were safe as a group seemed to bring back courage they were somewhat lacking. Just as the sun's last few rays disappeared behind the grain elevators, the boys were all hunkered down in some larges bushes near the trees. They had a clear view of both graves.

"By the way, just what are we suppose to do if we do see these ghosts?" Gary asked.

"We aren't, or should I say, we can't do anything. Just watch them, that's all," Charlie said.

"Boy, I wish one of us had brought a camera. Wouldn't it be great to take a picture of a couple ghosts to the Chickasha paper? That would make us about the most famous guys in Oklahoma. No, forget Oklahoma, we would be the most famous guys in America," Gary said, smiling at the others.

"Apparently, you've lost your ever-loving mind, Gary. 'Cause everyone knows you can't take pictures of ghosts. It's just as plain as the nose on one's face 'cause when you snap the picture, all the electrons or picture waves—or whatever waves the camera sends out—go right through a ghost 'cause ghosts are hollow. All a person can see of a ghost is a ghost cloud," Charlie answered.

"How, pray tell, do you know so much about ghosts?" Gary asked Charlie.

"I'll tell you how, because it's a known fact. Everyone knows that a known fact is something that is just known. It's something everyone knows. You just have to think about it and a known fact will just pop in your head. Well, if your head isn't hollow, that is," Charlie answered, hitting Gary on the shoulder and smiling.

"You guys better pipe down because I'll give you another known fact. A ghost will not appear if it knows someone is trying to catch a glimpse of it. I sure don't know a lot about ghosts but I am smart enough to know they like to be by themselves or, at least, with other ghosts," Sonny said.

They sat waiting for something to happen for several minutes before Jake asked, "Wonder why they are hanging around here and didn't just go straight up to heaven?"

"I was thinking on that myself," Charlie answered.

After a few seconds, Bruce whispered in what was definitely not a whisper. He asked aloud, "Well?"

"Well, it's like this. Them two were lovers here on earth. I figure they was mighty in love so when they died, an angel came down to them and said, 'Okay, here's the deal. You two are dead now, and I am here to fetch you guys to heaven'," Charlie said.

"An angel would never use the word *fetch*. When you become an angel, they also become all-knowing. And an all-knowing angel would never use *fetch* like some old hillbilly," Sonny said; this time, giving Charlie a little shove.

"Okay, anyway, I figured right then and there that boy Rick turned to his girlfriend and asked her thoughts on the matter. Being newly dead, they wasn't real sure how things went. So one of them had to ask the angel what it would be like being in heaven. Could they still get married and be in love and all up there?" Charlie looked around, trying to see the others' faces in the dark. "Anyways, I don't know a lot about heaven and all. But do you remember when that woman came to our church? I think her name was Lott. Been so long ago, I barely remember," Charlie said.

"That's right, I remember that day. I tried to play sick so I wouldn't have to go but my grandmother made me anyway," Sonny said.

"Sure, she's the woman who got killed or had a heart attack and died or something. Anyhow, something killed her for several minutes before the doctors brought her back to life," Charlie added. "During the time she was dead, she spent that time in heaven. She told everyone in church that it was the most beautiful place, like a big flower garden all filled with love. She even got to meet the people who had passed on before her."

"Dadgumit, that would be cool. I would like to meet Babe Ruth and talk to all kinds of people we read about in history," Jake answered.

"Anyway, I bet the angel told them that once they got through the gates leading into heaven, they would no longer be in love like they were down here on earth. All they could do was walk around, talk to all their dead friends, pick flowers, and things like that," Charlie said. "Wonder if there are mosquitoes and bees in heaven? Wouldn't it be the pits to die and go to heaven and have to put up with mosquitoes?" Bruce asked, laughing to himself.

"Work with me here, will you? Anyway, I bet Rick and Ernestine didn't think too highly of that so they just opted to hang around here as ghosts and continue to be lovers," Charlie finished.

"Are you trying to tell us that once they appear, they will be kissing and hugging and stuff like that?" Jake asked.

"Wouldn't surprise me. If they passed up a free trip to heaven to stay down here and be lovers, then why wouldn't they want to kiss hug and all that?" Charlie asked, looking around at the dark faces.

"What if they start doing more than kissing? I don't think it would be right to watch them having sex. That would make us peeping toms. What if they saw us, group or no group, they might come after us for peeping on them," Bruce said.

"My gosh! Don't any of you guys have any learning? Your parents send you to school to get you some learning and all you do is chew on the back of your books," Charlie answered.

"Ghosts don't make love. They just kiss and hug, that's all. Did you not understand when I said they was hollow? Hollow ghosts can't make love. They can just kiss and hug, that's it. Nothing more, nothing less," Charlie answered, with a little uncertainly in his voice.

"Look," Bruce whispered, pointing toward the two graves in the darkness.

All the boys' eyes were on both graves, expecting to see Rick and Ernestine come slowly up out of the ground.

Each boy seemed to move a little closer to each other until they were all as close as men in a football huddle. Their breathing became as one. A breath out of turn might just call one of the ghosts down on that person not in sync with the other four. Charlie felt the hand on his shoulder before he heard the words.

"What the hell are you boys doing here?"

Bruce let out a little scream. Jake fell forward, hiding his head with his arms. Sonny froze in place, as did Charlie and Gary.

"I'll ask you one more time. What are you boys doing here?" Mr. Troop demanded.

When the boys finally realized it wasn't the ghost of Rick or Ernestine talking to them, they turned around to see Mr. Troop standing behind them.

Shaking, Sonny said, "We were told that the graves are haunted. We were just trying to see if that was true or not."

"May I make a suggestion to you, boys?" Mr. Troop asked.

"Yes, sir," they seemed to all chime in together.

"Well, I suggest that if you boys want to see any ghost hunting, the best place would be the graveyard. I believe you fellows would have a much better chance to see a ghost in a place where there is hundreds of graves compared to only two," he said. All five of the boys nodded their heads up and down, agreeing with him. "And besides, how would I know if ghost hunting was what was really on your mind? Me being a father of two young girls, I might think you were here to spy on them," he said, looking from one to the other.

Four of the heads started shaking back and forth, while Jake was nodding his head yes. When he realized what he was doing, he changed to match that of the other four boys.

"Okay, boys, don't you think it's about time you all started for home?" Mr. Troop suggested.

With their heads nodding up and down, the boys took off toward town in a fast walk. Then, once away from Mr. Troop, they broke into a dead run. When they were far enough away, they stopped to catch their breath.

Sonny said, "You know this ghost hunting sure hasn't turned out anything like we planned last year. Now this year, we are getting caught by Mr. Troop. I think it's time to hang up ghost hunting."

Again, like clockwork, the others heads started to nod up and down in agreement.

5

One afternoon, Sonny, Jake, and Charlie were sitting in the park talking about girls, of all things. Not two years ago, they could not have cared less if there were girls alive on earth. At thirteen, most of them started to notice girls more and more. Now at fourteen, not only did they notice them, they even started to like being around them and didn't really care who knew it.

"You guys think Heather Porch is cute?" Jake asked, not looking at either of the other two. He just, more or less, said it to whichever of them might pick up on the question.

"Yes," Charlie answered.

Sonny chimed in. "Why you ask anyway?"

"Well, I was at the drugstore couple of days ago, picking something up for my folks when I met her coming out. She smiled at me. Then out of the blue, she started to talk to me about something or other—school play or something like that. I just can't remember," he said, smiling.

"No, you can't remember because you were so dumb-founded that a girl as pretty as Heather would even look at you, much less actually speaks to you," Sonny said.

"Isn't that the truth? No girl in her right mind would want to have anything to do with someone as homely as you," Charlie said, smiling and hitting Sonny on the shoulder.

"Come on, guys. I'm trying to be serious here," Jake said to the others, now laughing.

"Ha ha. I thought you were wearing a Halloween mask the first time I saw you," Sonny said. "There you were, walking into first grade and wearing a suit and tie. I remember wondering why that boy was wearing a suit and tie and that Frankenstein mask to his first day of school," Sonny said between laughs.

"My mother made me wear that stupid suit. She said it would make a good impression on the teacher and other kids," Jake answered, now smiling himself.

"Well, your mother was right about that. We boys, heck, everyone in the classroom that day thought, 'Wow, look at the dork with the suit on!'," Charlie answered.

"Ha ha. Anyway, Heather asked me if I would like to come over tonight and watch *The Andy Griffith Show* with her," he said, with a shy grin on his face.

"What did you tell her?" Charlie asked.

"What the heck do you think I told her? Good Lord, it's Heather Porch! I told her, 'Sure, I had nothing better to do'," he answered.

R. J. Burroughs

"Nothing better to do? That's no way to answer a girl. You should have said something like, 'My dear, wild animals couldn't keep me from your door'," Sonny answered, laughing out loud.

"Think we should tell him about the giant?" Charlie asked.

"No, let him find out for himself," Sonny answered.

"Tell me about what giant? Who's the giant?" Jake asked.

"Well, I guess we should. After all, he is one of us," Sonny said.

"The giant is Heather's dad, Mr. Porch. The story goes, they moved to Verden from Dallas because a lot of the young boys from his neighborhood came up missing. And the strangest part is, they were all young boys that he caught talking to Heather," Charlie said.

"That's bullcrap!" Jake answered.

"No, Jake, he is absolutely right. His name is Hal, and he is as big as a mountain. I once saw him pick up the back of a 1955 Chevy just to get one of Heather's ping pong balls out from under it," Sonny said.

"You guys are just ragging me. There is no man alive who can pick up the back of a car," Jake said, laughing with the others.

"You remember Tommy Oder? Well, I was told he went over there to have supper with Heather about a year ago. In fact, it was just about this time of the year," Sonny said.

"I remember Tommy. Wasn't he the kid that took fake chocolate chips cookies to the church on Wednesday pot luck?" Jake asked.

"That's him," Sonny answered.

"What about him and cookies?" Charlie asked.

"First, let me say Tommy was a nice boy. He did have his little differences but then, I guess we all have different ways in one way or another. I guess Tommy's just stood out more than most. One thing he really liked was to sing. Whenever you saw him walking down the street or in one of the stores in town, he would be singing some song. Now don't get me wrong, I like songs just as much as the other fellow but when Tommy sang, dogs and cats would run and hide. If there happened to be anyone sitting on their porch, they would go back inside as fast as they could and shut their doors and windows just as quickly. His singing was so bad," Sonny said, looking from one to the other. "I was told by Mr. Plumee that one time, Tommy was walking to the river to do some fishing. On his way down, he walked by Mr. Cline's dairy farm. That day, all seventy-three of his milk cows were grazing by the dirt road. Tommy was just walking on, singing his head off. Not only did his singing cause a stampede of all seventy-three of them cows, for a whole month, those milk cows dried up. Mr. Cline wasn't able to get one single drop of milk out of any of those cows."

"Mr. Plumee told you that? Sounds like a made-up story to me," Jake said. Even Charlie nodded his head in agreement with Jake.

"Nope, I'll have you know Mr. Plumee is the preacher at the Seventh Day Adventist church. And you know as well as I do, no preacher from any Adventist church would ever tell a lie or even so much as fib to anyone," Sonny said.

"Well, how about that Adventist preacher in Anadarko that took off with all the church money as well as one of the member's wife?" Jake asked.

"Well, I bet he wasn't really a preacher. I bet he cheated on his preacher test they give before you can be called preacher," Sonny answered.

"I have never heard of any preacher test. I think you just have to be voted in to be a preacher," Charlie answered.

"Well, it makes no difference. Anyway, Tommy also had a fast temper. That's why he took the cookies to the Wednesday night church supper the Adventists like to have," Sonny said. "Seems the Wednesday night before the cookies, everyone finished eating their chicken or casseroles or whatever was brought to church that night. Then Tommy decided he would get up on the little stage and serenade everyone with a version of a song he wrote or, should I say, made-up in his head. So without a by-your-leave or kiss-my-butt, Tommy jumps up on the stage and starts singing.

> I woke up this morning, feeling rejected, feeling alone
> I called on my Savior, ask him a favor, help me carry
> my burdens along
> Then he came to me. Yes, he came to me
> With power of the ocean, the strength of the sea.

"Before he could sing the next verse, people started to place their hands over their ears, some made awful faces. A few of the teenagers even started to boo. Apparently, the preacher walked up to Tommy on stage and politely asked him to please stop singing. He was afraid that so soon after everyone had just eaten, this singing might just cause a few of them to toss up what they just ate. Course, being a preacher and all, I am sure he used a word like *regurgitate*, trying to spare Tommy's feelings just a little bit. But the damage had been done by then, no matter if he had used *toss up* or not. Like I said, Tommy had a heck of a temper. It's a wonder he didn't fly off the handle or something. But Tommy slowly stepped off the stage, went back to his chair, calmly picked up what was left of a chicken leg he had been eating, and started to nibble on it again. If anyone had chosen to look closely at Tommy, they would have seen slight tears in the corner of each eye. The tears were not tears of sadness, but tears of anger," Sonny said, looking first to Jake then to Charlie.

"Well, what did he do? Did he stop going to church on Wednesdays?" Jake asked.

"Gosh, no. He went on like it never happened. But when he got home from church that night, he went straight to his bedroom and broke open his piggybank. It contained something like fifty-seven dollars and sixty-two cents. The next morning, Tommy went to the grocery store in town and bought all the chocolate chip cookies the store had, which turned out to be eleven packs of cookies. Next, he went to the drugstore and bought twenty-two boxes of

Aunt Door's chocolate stool softener. Tommy wasn't seen around town much that week. People that knew him figured he was upset about how he was treated that night. They figured that in a few days, he would be back to walking around town, singing as usual. But, the real reason Tommy was not seen was because he was home in his room with his pocketknife, digging the little chocolate chips out of each cookie. He replaced the chocolate chips with the chocolate from Aunt Door's stool softener. Each time he finished a pack of cookies, he would stick that pack in the oven on a low temperature to melt the chocolate in place," Sonny said, smiling.

"I know what is coming next." Jake laughed.

"Yes, you are right, Jake. That next Wednesday, he took all the cookies and covered them with tinfoil on a large green serving plate. He placed the cookie plate at the back of the church for people to grab and eat when they came in and while the preacher preached the Wednesday night sermon. The sermon lasted about an hour and fifteen minutes, just the time needed for Aunt Door's stool softener to get a good hold of everyone's digestive system. In the middle of the Wednesday night meal, not only was there lines to the men's and women's bathrooms, but a couple of the older people just couldn't hold their bowels. Mary Ann Mayo was waiting in line to the bathroom when she could no longer hold it. She lost her bowels as she ran for the exit. The preacher and a few of the wives also lost control, watching

Mary Ann. Everyone was running for the exit toward a stand of trees at the back of the church. It had to be a funny sight, seeing all the women with their dresses pulled up and the men on the other side with their pants down. Tommy, being the good Christian that he was, went around handing one square of toilet paper to each man, woman, and child. It was later called the running squats. For several months, there was a terrible smell coming from the wooded area. In fact, if the wind was just right, church services had to be canceled because of the stink," Sonny finished.

"What does this have to do with my going to Heather's house?" Jake asked.

"Well, after Tommy went over there, he was only seen a couple of times in town. And he never sang again. So one can only imagine what Mr. Porch did to him. Lord, I'm scared to even imagine what could have happened," Charlie said.

"All we can say is, good luck, Jake," Sonny added.

6

Jake wanted to call Heather to give her some reason why he wouldn't be able to come over that night but he really had no good reason for not going. He thought about telling her that his mother just passed away but if Heather saw his mother at the store or someplace else in the next day or two, then that would give his lie away. Heather would never want to talk to him again. And if Heather was to tell his mom the lie he told to get out of seeing her, well...there was no telling if his mom would let him live or not. He really wanted to go over but after what Charlie and Sonny told him about her dad, he was more than a little hesitant. In fact, he was scared. He just hoped that when he got the courage to go, he wouldn't show how scared he was.

Walking to her house, something else started to bother him. He had never been to a girl's house before. With each step he took, he tried to think of what he would say to her. With the way he felt, he wasn't sure if he would even be able to talk. He stood at the screen door for a couple of seconds before he knocked. He could see the house through the screen because of the bright lights inside. Swallowing several times, he knocked on the door. It seemed like forever before anyone came.

Then, all of a sudden, he thought they must have turned off the lights because all the brightness coming through the door seemed to cease in an instant. Then he knew why. Heather's dad was standing there. He wasn't near as big as Jake expected; he was a lot bigger. He was big enough to block out all the light coming from the door.

"You must be Jake," he said.

Jake was so much in awe of him he couldn't speak.

"Well, boy, are you Jake or just some kid selling cookies?" Hal said to him, trying not to smile.

"No, sir, I'm not selling cookies," Jake finally answered.

"Well, what are you doing here?" he asked.

For the first time in his life, Jake couldn't seem to speak.

Then just like the medics in wars that saved so many of our wounded boys, Heather pushed her father a little bit out of the way and said, "Hi, Jake. This is my dad, Hal. Won't you come in? Andy Griffith will be on in a few minutes."

Heather's dad moved just enough to let Jake slide by him. Jake and Heather went into the front room. She motioned for him to sit on the couch and sat down beside him. Heather's father sat in the La-Z-Boy across the room from the two of them. Jake watched him. He knew the chair was an inanimate object but he still felt sorry for the La-Z-

Boy. The two kids made small talk about school, things that went on around town, and some of the friends they had in common while waiting for the Andy Griffith show to come on. Jake had a hard time keeping up with the conversation as he kept looking at her father, who was staring at him from across the room. Jake had no idea how that La-Z-Boy could hold up such a massive man. The man showed no fat and was about ninety percent muscle.

To make matters even worse, Heather was wearing a short black tight skirt, and when she sat down beside him, it came halfway up her thighs. Jake tried not to look at her legs as they watched television but that was about as easy as finding chicken lips in the meat department in the local supermarket. It was something that just couldn't be done. As Opie was getting scolded by Andy for shooting a bird, Jake looked down at Heather's legs for about the twentieth time. This time, when he looked up, he saw Hal. Hal's eyes were not on the television at all. His eyes were glued on Jake, watching his every move. Jake wished the show would be over. He felt like he was a marine behind enemy lines, about to be caught stealing top-secret papers. In his case, the papers were the enemy's daughter's legs.

During the commercial, Hal said to Jake, "My wife, Kimberly, won't let me have my cigar in the house. How about going out back with me while I catch a few puffs?"

Jake figured this was it. Her dad had seen him looking at his daughter's legs all those times. Now he was either going to kill him or, at the very least, break several of his bones.

They walked out back together while Mr. Porch lit a cigar that looked as if he had smoked and relit it several times. Jake sat down in one of the lawn chairs that were on the back porch.

"What you planning on doing after school?" Hal asked.

Jake looked up at him kind of dumbfounded. Here he was, fourteen years old, and this was the first time anyone had ever asked him that. He started to say he had no idea but stopped short of that. He wanted, of all people, for Heather's dad to think he had ambitions, that he wanted to make something of himself. "I am leaving my options open on that, sir. I was thinking about becoming a doctor or lawyer, but I feel I have several more years before I have to decide," he said, feeling good about his answer.

"Well, we better get back in to see what Andy does to Opie about that bird he shot," Mr. Porch said to Jake. "But before we go in, I think we have time for me to show you something," he said, smiling.

Jake thought he was about to be taken to the bushes and murdered. He figured Mr. Porch had a baseball bat hidden in the bushes, somewhere out there in the dark night, to beat him to death. How would his folks take it when they found his body had been bludgeoned plumb to death.

"Look here, Jake," Mr. Porch said, pointing to a hole in the ground. The hole was about three feet deep and five feet long.

Looking at the hole, Jake thought it looked a lot like a grave—a grave that was just about the right size for a fourteen-year-old boy. "Nice hole," was all Jake could think to say.

"You know, boy, I sure love my daughter. If anyone was to hurt her, I have no idea what I would be capable of doing to that person," he said.

Once back in the house on the couch next to Heather, Jake didn't once look at her legs. When the show was over, Heather asked if he would like to go sit on the back porch and talk. He told her he thought he might have caught diabetes walking over. He figured he better get home, take a couple of aspirins, and go right to bed to see if he couldn't sleep the diabetes off.

Standing on the porch, Heather leaned over and gave him a kiss on the cheek. She thanked him for coming over. When he felt her lips on his cheek, it was like that can of spinach that Popeye the Sailor Man takes for strength. That kiss did something to him and made him feel something he had never felt before.

"You know, Heather, I think my sugar diabetes has gone away. If you still want to, I would sure like to set on the back porch and talk for awhile," he said to her.

They sat and talked for almost an hour before Kimberly sent him home. In that hour with her, he could not have cared less if he was about to be bludgeoned to death or stuffed in that hole in the backyard. All he cared about was talking to her. If he was lucky, he might get another kiss on his cheek when he left again for the night. Who's to know, she might even let him kiss her on the lips. He knew as good as a kiss felt on his cheek, one planted square on the lips might take him right straight into manhood. He just couldn't wait to tell the others about the kiss and the effect it had on him. He figured he wouldn't say a word about looking at her legs most of the night. They might think him a pervert for not watching the show and only trying to sneak a peek of Heather's legs. He sure didn't want to have the tag *pervert* hung on him like old man Buckner.

Jake remembered when he first heard the word *pervert*. His mother said, "Well, they caught the sock pervert. Of all people, it was Mr. Buckner. He's the man who does most of the welding in town for people as well as work on small engines." Jake asked her just what in the heck a *pervert* was. "Well, boy, a pervert is some fellow that does some mighty strange things."

"You mean, like the fellow that throws cucumbers at funerals?" Jake asked her.

"No, that guy is nothing more than a nutcase. He has several screws loose. Wouldn't surprise me one bit if he has more screws loose than tight. Anyone that goes around throwing cucumbers at a hearse with some poor deceased person in it has to be smooth off their rocker," she said to him, with a frown on her face. "No, boy, a pervert is usually a person that does crazy weird stuff that is more or less in a sexual way. Course, I guess it could also be other ways but for the life of me, I have never heard of any."

"Is that what Mr. Buckner did, something in a sexual manner?" he asked her.

"Well, Mr. Buckner liked to prowl around at night and take things off people's clotheslines," she answered.

"That sounds more like a thief to me," Jake answered.

"Well, yes, I guess it does. Except, he only took black socks and girls' black undergarments. Nothing more. Mr. Buckner is a pretty good-size man so he sure wasn't able to wear the socks and he would never fit into a pair of black panties. So that makes him a pervert. A clothes pervert," she answered.

No, Jake decided he would never tell the guys about looking at her legs. He didn't want to be marked as a pervert by his friends—or anyone else, for that matter. He sure had no reason to be taking anyone's socks or any girls' underwear.

7

Sonny was walking to the drugstore to pick up some Garrett snuff for his grandmother when Bruce came running up to him saying, "The McGills are leaving for Chickasha this morning. I guess Mr. McGill's brother, Mark, passed away last night in the Chickasha hospital," Bruce said.

The boys always liked Mark. He was a really nice guy. Of course, he was a little off his rocker. Well, a *lot* off his rocker would better describe him. Mark didn't like cats. If he happened to see a cat walking toward him, he would move to the other side of the street. If that cat came across the street, Mark would just turn and run. It made no difference to Mark how long or how far he had to run to get away from the cat, as long as he got away. The boys once saw him running across Highway 62, dodging cars as he went. People who didn't know Mark would have thought someone was after him. Townfolks who knew him would just turn to one another and say "Cat," and go about their business.

Mark had another little hang-up. He was scared to death of anyone from a country other than the United States. Once, he rode over to Chickasha with a couple of friends to watch the rodeo. They stopped to get some Coke and stuff to eat because buying things at the rodeo was way too expensive for their taste and, more importantly, their wallet. Mark had a couple bags of chips, two candy bars, and a sixteen-ounce Coke when he walked up to pay. The cashier was an old guy from Pakistan who could barely speak English. He tried to say, "This everything?" Before he could finish the word *everything*, Mark dropped the things he was carrying and ran for the door. He ran all eight miles back to Verden. The boys he came with tried to get him back in the car but Mark would have nothing to do with that. He just kept running. Other than that, he was always willing to help anyone with anything. When he found out he had stomach cancer, it didn't change him one bit. He just kept on trying to help others anyway he could.

When he passed away, it affected most everyone in town, as there wasn't anyone around he had not helped, one way or the other. The day of the funeral, the boys put on the best clothes they had other than their Sunday suits. They knew that Mark had never seen them in suits, and they wanted to dress like he remembered them. It was kind of a surprise that there weren't more people at the funeral. There were no more than fifteen or twenty folks. For some reason, the preacher, who was going to do the services, had the few that came sit in special places. That seemed strange to the boys but then, they hadn't been to that many funerals in their fourteen years of life. The fact being, the grownups always thought the boys were way too young to go to funerals. They figured it might stunt their growth or cause them to have nightmares. The one funeral they did attend was for one of their friend's sister who was struck by lightning. It was sad, that's for sure, but none of them had nightmares. If the parents were worried about nightmares, they should have stopped the boys from going to see *The Creature from the Black Lagoon*. They had nightmares for weeks, and, in fact, none of them would go out in the dark alone for about the same length of time.

As they sat waiting for the funeral to start, Jake said, "Wouldn't it be cool if Mark was alive? If he was just doing this to see who would show up?"

"Well, if he is alive and I go up to his casket and he reaches up and grabs me, then I will need a new pair of pants. And that's a fact. Do you remember the Zombie thing we went through a couple years ago right here? Well, I sure as heck do not want to go through that again. Instead of just getting knocked out, I am sure I would have a heart attack," Sonny said.

"Well, at least you would already be at the funeral home," Bruce whispered.

Charlie was just about to say something about sonny having a heart attack when he changed his mind and instead said, "Look, isn't that Mark's ex-wife?"

All the boys turned their heads real slow to see Linda McKee walking in, wearing a long black dress with her head covered by a black veil. You could tell her appearance at her ex-husband's funeral was a surprise to everyone. Some people smiled at her. You could tell the smiles on their faces were not really what they would like to show this woman but protocol at a funeral called for everyone to be civil.

The only person allowed to not be civil to other people would be Mark but he was way past being civil to anyone. Mark was either in glory land or on his way to glory land. The boys weren't sure if a person went to glory before their funeral or if they left right after the funeral. When the preacher saw Mark's ex-wife, Linda, walking down the aisle, he jumped up and escorted her to the seat he had prepared for her if she happened to show up. The sermon lasted about ten minutes. The preacher said a few things about how Mark always liked to help others that he would give the shirt off his back to help a stranger.

Jake whispered to Sonny, "You know, it seems whenever someone dies, that person would always give the shirt off their back to help others. Even if the dead guy or girl was a bank robber, a murderer, or one of them perverts, I think all preachers all over the world have to say that for some reason."

"I guess they teach that in preacher school. You wouldn't want the preacher saying things like, 'Wow, sure glad this fellow is gone! He was nothing but a butthead. He would steal the shirt right off your back if you didn't watch him. Now, let's all thank the Lord he is gone on to his reward, whatever that reward might be'," Sonny answered with a big grin on his face.

"I guess that's true. I guess, it wouldn't do to say something like that with his friends and family all setting around crying and all," Jake answered.

After a couple of songs were played over the speaker, Mr. Hanson, the funeral director, came out and walked to the casket. He smiled at the people then turned and proceeded to open the small lid of the casket, exposing Mark's upper torso.

"Damn," Bruce said, leaning back against the pew.

There was Mark, laid in a white suit and red tie. He looked like he was about to go to a sock hop or be the emcee at the state fair, not on his way to glory land.

"What's wrong with you, Jake?" Charlie asked. "You look like someone just took a pee in you oatmeal."

"Nothing wrong. I was just wondering when a fellow stands up before God, will they be wearing whatever it is they were buried in? If so, the good Lord should get a good laugh when Mark shows up in that getup," he answered.

After the music had stopped, Mr. Hanson said they could now pass by the casket and say their goodbyes to

Mark for the last time. Mr. Hanson made it clear that they were to file by the casket in the same order as he had them seated. The first person to walk by was Larry Powers, the usher at the movie theater. When Larry was only a couple of feet away opposite Mark, a *click* came over the speaker system in the room.

"Hi, Larry, I am so glad you came. I just wanted to tell you that you sure suck as a movie usher," came the words from a recording Mark must have made just before he died.

Sonny looked at Jake then the others. There was a look at first of terror then big smiles. You could see each boy was doing his best to not laugh out loud.

Next was Betty Black, the teller at the Verden Bank. Again, Mark's voice came on. "Hi, Betty. I always wanted to tell you just how pretty I thought you were. Course, I was always afraid to say anything to you. So, Betty, you're mighty pretty and you have one fine figure. I thought about you nearly every night just before I went to sleep."

You could see Betty was eating this up by the big smile that crossed her face. The boys figured Mr. Hanson was pushing a button to play a prerecorded message each time the right person got near Mark to pay their last respects. Next came Rose Ford, one of the checkers at the grocery store. When she approached the casket, she stood there for a few seconds but nothing happened. Mark must not have recorded anything for her. You could see the disappointment on her face as she looked up at the speakers. Then came Richard Gholson, a retired police officer from town.

"Hi, Richard," the recorder sounded. "Remember that time you wouldn't let me go for speeding down Main Street? I was going only one mile an hour over the speed limit. Well, I started to have Mr. Hanson put me in this box facedown so you could kiss my butt. I have about as much respect for you as I would one of them little tics I've pulled off my dog's butt." You could hear the *click* as the recorder was shut off.

That did it for the boys. They tried to control their laughter but were unable to do so. All five of them started to laugh out loud.

Then came Angie Harris. Angie was an older woman who everyone in town knew spent every waking hour hunting for a husband or going to funerals for something to do. Her first husband had just up and disappeared. One day, he was working on Mr. Benda's farm as a handyman; the next thing, he was gone. Angie said she thought there was foul play going on but everyone in town knew he had taken off. It only took about one minute for a normal person to get a gutful of Angie. Her husband had been married to her for three years so everyone figured he had to beat it to save what sanity he had left. When Angie stood in front of the casket, the recorder came to life. "Angie, one of the good things about being dead is I won't have to hear you asking me over to your home for supper anymore. Let me tell you, when your day comes to enter heaven, if you happen to see me hanging around this or that—or wherever there is to hang around in heaven, that is—please don't come talk to me. I don't want to be your man or be around you, even way the hell up there." *Click*, the recorder went silent again.

Charlie put his hands over his mouth but he just couldn't control the laughter. A few of the people attending the funeral looked at him but most all of them were grinning from ear to ear. Charlie was the only one that made any kind of noise with his laughing.

Next came his ex-wife, Linda McKee. Linda had been married to Mark for about three years before she and her boss became lovers. A month or two after that, Linda told Mark she thought they should separate. She really wanted to get away from him to be her boss's mistress. If anyone ever said anything bad about her, Mark would always take up for her. They all thought he figured she would smarten up and come back one day since her boss was married. However, that never happened. Linda walked up to the casket, holding a white hanky to her nose and mouth.

The boys thought they could hear a whimper or two coming from behind the veil that was covering her face. The boys would have given just about anything they owned, which wasn't much, if they could just see her face. They didn't know if the whimpers were actually small laughs trying to be muffled or if she was really sad Mark was off to points unknown. They couldn't figure how she could be sad after all the things she put him through in his life.

She stood there for what seemed like several minutes. It was long enough that the boys figured he didn't think she would attend his funeral so he didn't bother to record anything to her.

Then just as she was about to turn to walk away, they heard that *click*. They were on the edge of the pew, not wanting to miss hearing anything that was about to be said to the one woman in his life that treated him so poorly.

"Well, Linda, I wasn't sure you would be here. I wonder if you are here from guilt or in hopes the money I had saved might be coming to you. Linda, I waited all my life for you to come back and I can say *all my life* being where I am right now. Anyway, now I can say I wasted that time because you were not worth waiting on. When I get up there with the good old Lord himself, I will try my best to persuade him to give you and your lover a case of the continuous runner's trots. I would love to sit up there and watch you get crapped on every day and every night for the rest of your life, just like you crapped on me. As for the money I have left, I have given that to the Salvation Army. So if you want any of that money, you best stand in front of some store around Christmas time and ring that little bell with that red pot in front of you, then they might pay you for doing that with some of the money I donated to them." *Click.* Everything went dead once again.

Linda didn't even walk back to her seat. She turned and walked straight out of the side door.

The people in attendance were looking from one to the other. A couple of the women's mouths were so wide open that Gary thought they looked like a couple of largemouth bass he caught a few times, wide open as they were. The boys weren't sure but they thought they heard a few people clapping from somewhere in the church. The only person who lost it completely was Mr. Hanson. He stood behind the casket, laughing out loud. You could tell he wanted to stop laughing but just couldn't control it. It had the better of him.

When it was the boys' time to go up and pay their respects, Mr. Hanson had all five of them come up together. *Click.* "Well, boys, of all the people who came to see me off to the land way up yonder, I knew you five would be here. As many good times we all had together of me telling you stories, I will be looking down on you boys. I will do my best to watch over all of you. Course, I may have to ask Leroy Mayhue to help me with that task, as many things you boys seem to get into all of the time. So take care." *Click.* It went silent again.

As they were walking back to their pew, the recorder clicked on again. They heard Mark's voice for the last time. He said, "And any of you I might not have spoken to, I would like to say one more thing. And that is 'Wow, don't I look like myself?' Now go out unto the multitude and tell all the people who didn't come to see me off, 'Boy, he sure did look like himself.'" They heard Mark started to laugh. Then *click*, it was silent.

That did it. Some of the people broke out in laughter, and those who didn't laugh out loud were snickering to themselves.

8

The afternoon following the funeral, the boys met at the train depot. Mr. Burger said he would tell them another story about a couple of brothers who used to live in Verden. As always, Mr. Burger leaned back in his chair and put his feet up next to the telegraph key. He wanted to be nearby if a message happened to come in so he could attend to it.

"Boys, ten or twenty years ago—I'm not real sure just how long ago it was—anyway, there was a couple of brothers that lived out to where Lake Chickasha is nowadays. You know, that's a man-made lake. Don't rightly remember what year the dam was built. But before it was built, all that was there was what a person could call an old large pond," he said, as he started getting into his story. "In those days, the Roe brothers lived close to the pond before they turned it into Lake Chickasha. Let's see, the oldest brother was Cleo, the younger of the two was Ro-Ro. He was, I figure, 'bout nine months younger than Cleo. Never could figure out why the name Ro-Ro or even how to write it down if the need ever came up. Thankfully, it never did."

He continued, "It's hard for me to remember but I think the reason they was so close to the same age and not being twins was because they were conceived toward the end of the dust bowl. When one of those dust clouds showed up, it might be a few hours to a day or more that a fellow couldn't leave his house because of the dust blowing around blinding you. In fact, Buck and Judy Lilly took off to town one afternoon when a hell of a duster showed up. You know, boys, they were never seen again. You can believe that or not but it's a pure fact. Was nothing a person could do during the dust storm, except stay in the house because the dust was so darn thick. It was so thick that if a fellow didn't put some kind of a rag or something over their mouth or nose, that dust would plug them plumb up. So staying in the house was the thing to be doing in those duster days. That, sure enough, gave men and women lots of extra time to conceive," he said, with a big grin on his old wrinkled face.

"Conceive?" Charlie asked, looking around at the others.

"Don't you got yourself no education?" Jake said, trying to talk like a hillbilly.

"You need to pay more attention in biology class, Charlie," Sonny said, smiling at the boys and Mr. Burger.

"Means that's how Cleo and Ro-Ro's mom got in the motherly way, you goofball,"

Bruce said.

"Anyways, apparently, the boys' mother was a real untrusting soul. I believe the reason she didn't trust people was because her husband came to Verden to pick up something or other one morning. I don't know what he came to town to get. Some people have told me it was a piece for his plow," Mr. Burger said, looking toward the ceiling and scratching the back of his head. "Anyway, back to the story, Mr. Roe never made it back home. Last anyone seen of him, he was standing outside the Gulf station on Highway 62. In those days, the Greyhound bus stopped at that station each day around noon. Most people figured he just decided to leave all his troubles behind. He must have just got on that Greyhound bus and left for points unknown." Mr. Burger was nodding his head to what he just said. "Mrs. Roe was sure one of them little blood veins in his brain, which supply blood to the area of the brain that makes a man remember he is married and has a family, just up and exploded. She figured that's when that happened, the lack of blood going to that part of his brain caused him to forget who he was and even where he came from. For some reason, we seem to have a lot of folks from Verden over the years who just up and leave, never to be heard of again."

Mr. Burger listened to the telegraph key clicking. Deciding it wasn't for him, he continued with his story. "I believe, as well as a lot of other people around here believed, that he just up and left or he found another woman, or something like that, after what happened to Lillian Elbert," he said, leaning back in his chair.

"Who is Lillian Elbert?" Bruce asked.

Sonny had to grin to himself, thinking how Mr. Burger could run stories together. Yet before he finished, everything seemed to fit together most times.

"She was the switchboard lady, back several years ago," he answered.

"What did she do and how does she fit into this story?" Jake asked, sitting down on the floor and leaning his back against the opposite wall.

"Just hang in there, boys. I'll explain everything as we go along," he answered. "Well, if I remember correctly, it happened one Saturday morning. That morning, Lillian, for some reason unknown to God or anyone else in town, plugged everyone in Verden into her switchboard at the same time. Back then, I believe all she had to do was pull all the little wires out of some panel and plug them all into the little holes. Each hole on her board was someone in town's phone. In many cases, one hole might take care of four or five families if those families were all on a party line together." You could tell this really perked up the boys' attention. Everyone on the phone at once sounded like something really funny to them. "Anyway, once she had everyone on the line, she started screaming that someone had stolen her husband," he said smiling.

"Had someone really run off with her husband?" Charlie asked.

"Why, Lord, no. She was never married. No man in his right mind would ever ask Lillian to get married. She was too darn mean," Mr. Burger said, rubbing his forehead with the back of his hand. "When a person picked up his or her phone, asked her to connect you to this person or that person, you never knew what her responses might be. I tried to get her to ring up my wife one afternoon. I wanted to ask Mrs. Burger what was for supper. Good Lord, you would have thought I asked Lillian for her dress size or what color panties she had on the way she flew off the handle screaming at me. She said, 'Now, Burger,'—she liked to call people by their last name. I guess it made her feel like they were under her is about the only thing I could figure about that. 'Burger, now why in the name of the Lord do you want to call your wife? Don't they give you enough work keeping up with all them trains that come through town like Casey Jones himself was driving them? Or you think she is out with some other fellow or something? Or maybe you think I don't have something better to do with my time than ring your wife up because you just feel the need to check on her?' she said."

"Did she go ahead and call her anyway?" Sonny asked.

"Yes, but I am sure she listened in on the conversation because as I was telling my wife good-bye and I heard a cough in the background. That had to be her because she coughed something fearful from all the cigarettes she smoked each day." Mr. Burger stood up to stretch his legs. "I can't even count the number of times people would drive by the telephone office and see smoke coming out of one of the windows. Thinking the place was about to burn down, they would call the fire department. That smoke was nothing more than Lillian smoking. Heck, she would have one hanging out of her mouth with several others smoldering in ashtrays scattered about," he said, standing up again to get blood flowing better in his legs. "If I sit too long, my old legs seem to kind of cramp up." He did what looked like a little jig before sitting back down. "Could that woman ever smoke. More times than I can count, I saw her lighting a cigarette with the cigarette she was smoking at the time, one right after the other. Yep, she sure was one powerful smoker. Smoking will kill you, boys. So if someone was to offer you a cigarette, don't take it or you will end up like Lillian," he said, pulling a little step stool out from under his desk to prop his legs on. Apparently, he must have seen what appeared to be looks of wonderment on the faces looking up at him. "Yes, boys, smoking went and killed old Lillian graveyard dead. Fact is, she is in the graveyard right over there," he said, pointing out the window toward the hill where her grave was.

"She just started to cough one day, I first noticed it at church. She was setting about two pews behind me and my missus. Every few minutes, you could hear a little cough coming from her. As time went by, when people walked into church, they would look around for Lillian because no one wanted to sit anywhere near her. Her coughing disturbed them so much. I guess her coughing kept several of the men from sleeping," he said, laughing out loud. "Then one day, I was standing out front of the drugstore when Lillian walked by pulling a little oxygen bottle to help her breathe. And, if you can believe this, she was pulling the oxygen bottle with one hand while holding a lit cigarette in the other. Boys, it wasn't long after that I was paying my last respects to her in Mr. Hanson's funeral parlor. Most everyone thought the cancer in her lungs did her in, but the truth is—or I believe the truth is—she had a heck of an argument with some fellow at the bank about her being a lady and she should be first in the line. Apparently, whoever she had the argument with didn't feel the same. Made her so mad she stormed out of the bank in a dead run, pulling that little oxygen bottle behind her. She was moving so fast that one of them little wheels on the oxygen cart fell smooth off. I was told that didn't seem to bother her one iota. She just kept running and pulling that cart until she got to her front porch. That is where she fell smack on her face dead, like that old Custer fellow after them Indians got finished with him. I figure something in Lillian's head must have just exploded, like one of them cherry bombs you boys seem to like so much on 4th of July and just like the veins in Maud's husband's head could have just up and popped.

"But I digress. Apparently, Mrs. Roe—by the way, her Christian name was Maud— Maud must not put much store in that blood vein blowing up in her husband's head all that much because at any given time, she would pop up out of the blue someplace, trying to catch him at this place or that," Mr. Burger said, again grinning. "No one seems to know why Maud thought her husband was still in town hiding from her. The facts about old Maud, her showing up at this place or that place, became plumb creepy. You might be in the grocery store picking up a can of them refried beans or a can of cream corn then when you turned the corner of the aisle, there she would be, just staring at you. Maud got so strange looking for her husband that she might be squatting down behind the rack of bread or behind the Twinkies, hoping to surprise Mr. Roe if he showed up. When old Mr. Nolen passed away from old age and they had his body ready to view, most everyone from town went to the church at different times to pay their last respects, like folks do. Well, that Maud would hide in the baptismal, peeking out through the red curtains they pulled closed when it wasn't in use. Yes, there stood Maud, waist deep in the water, peeking out at the people paying their respects. It's just a wonder no one ever spotted her. Might have given them a heck of a case of the willies, seeing her eyes peeking out from behind those two curtains. I know it would have scared the pee-waddlin' soup out of me for sure," he laughed out loud. Maud never did catch her husband anywhere in

Verden but she did catch pneumonia from standing in the cold water in the baptismal all those hours waiting to catch him," he said, trying to stop laughing. "About a week or two after that, Mrs. Roe was laid up in her very own casket from the pneumonia she caught while on the hunt. When Maud passed on to glory land, she left her two boys all alone out there to fend for themselves."

Mr. Burger continued, "Now the good Lord knows I'm sure not the smartest fellow in town, nor am I the dumbest. The award for the dumbest has to go to Cleo and Ro-Ro. The boys took the cake when it came to doing dumb stuff. They decided that they kind of enjoyed going to church after attending their mother's funeral. It must have been the first time those two boys ever set foot in a church attending that funeral," he said, sticking his legs out in front of him, exercising them. "They enjoyed church so much that they started to attend Reverend Gee Phillips' congregation. Now you boys are way too young to remember the Reverend Phillips but let me tell you this, he was about as much of a preacher as I am a camel jockey—and I can't even remember ever seeing a live camel," he said, shaking his head back and forth again. "Reverend Phillips was nothing more than a shyster, if you were to ask me. I attended his church once because he would invite me every darn time I ran into him. So one Sunday, I went, if nothing more than to shut him up. In church, he talked about the Lord about five minutes and what he said was nothing but nonsense.

The Bible never said one thing about fried chicken that I know of. Anyways, the rest of the hour he asked and begged for money. I knew, right off the bat, this fellow was a pure fake. He only wanted money. He couldn't care less if a person's soul went to glory land or to hell, to England or to hobnob with the queen herself. "Like I said, Cleo and Ro-Ro were several grains short of a bushel. So everything that the reverend said from the podium, the two boys took it right to heart, thinking it was nothing but pure fact. I wasn't there, mind you, but I think Reverend Phillips must have said something about the world about to come to an end, like it says in the book of Revelations in the Bible. I figure as simple as those two boys were, they took it to heart that the world was truly ending in a day or two. Apparently, they took all the money their mother had left them out of the bank and bought all types of food. I'm told there wasn't one can of chicken soup left anywhere in town. It appeared that them boys really enjoyed chicken soup. They bought all the bread the store had in stock, something like forty or so loafs. Darn good thing they had distaste for brown bread so the rest of us could have at least the brown bread with our meals," he said, again laughing out loud.

"They bought up all the shells they could find for their guns. I guess they figured they could hold off all the critters it talks about in Revelations. I figure they thought they would just shoot anybody or anything that came around them and eat white bread soaked in chicken soup until they both grew old and died from natural causes," Mr. Burger, said shaking his legs again. "A few of the townsfolk got worried about them and went out there to check on them. They near got their heads blown smooth off. They called the sheriff but he said they had every right to protect their home from intruders. If they thought they could shoot it out with the Lord's angels and fend off Revelations, then more power to the boys." Mr. Burger sat up straight in his chair, stretching.

"To make a long story short, I guess all the food they stored up started to run out after a couple of months. As the story goes, when Cleo opened and ate the last can of soup without giving Ro-Ro any, it made Ro-Ro so mad he shot the big toe off Cleo's right foot. When Cleo went to jumping around and screaming from the pain, Ro-Ro shot his own toe off to make amends. They were both bleeding so bad they figured they were about to go into their own Revelations so they hopped to town, hanging on to one another. Seeing the boys in such shape, the sheriff first took them to the hospital in Chickasha then to the mental ward in Norman, which was the last anyone ever heard of the boys. There was a few rumors that went around for a year or two after the boys were gone. One was that they escaped from the hospital and are now living somewhere in New York City. Another one was they both fell in love with the nurse that took care of them. They talked her into leaving with them and now all three live in New Orleans, where they sell voodoo dolls on the street corner. Course, none of them ever panned out, however," he said, getting up at last and letting the boys know the story was over.

9

At age fourteen, it always pays for a boy to keep his eyes and ears open, especially in a small town like Verden. There was never any telling what a kid might overhear when the grown-ups were talking among themselves. If one of the boys happened to see a couple of grown-ups off to themselves, talking in whispers while looking around to see if they were being overheard, they figured that was cause enough to do their best, their duty, to find out what they were talking about. That's what happened with Jake one afternoon just outside the post office.

Jake saw Mr. Gentry and Mr. Gill talking in a whisper at the edge of the alley that ran next to the post office. Their whispering to one another was just as good as if one of the men was calling out to Jake, saying, "Boy, come over here and try to listen to what we are talking about. It may be the start of an adventure for you and your buddies."

Sure enough, it was. When Jake met up with the boys later, he said the two men were talking about Mrs. Milam, the cat lady that lived a block east of the water tower. When a person saw Mrs. Milam walking around town and they didn't know she was the cat lady, they would think she was just a sweet old grandmother. She walked around town a lot, carrying her old large black purse.

One afternoon while walking to town with his mother, Sonny made the mistake and brought up Mrs. Milam in conversation. She said, "Boy, you stay away from that old woman. Not only is she touched in her old head, but I'm told she is meaner than two tomcats tied together in a gunny sack."

The boys were not sure but they figured that Mrs. Milam must have several cats living with her. That's why people in town called her the cat lady. The men at the post office said no one had seen her around in several days; something that wasn't like her. Most any day, she could be seen walking around Verden carrying that big old purse of hers. They said if they didn't see her around town by the middle of next week, they would call the law to go check in on her. The boys figured that gave them four to five days tops to check on Mrs. Milam themselves but, they didn't need all that time. They decided they would sneak over to her house Friday night. On Fridays and Saturdays, the boys' folks would let them stay outside until 10:30 p.m. An extra thirty minutes wasn't all that much but to the boys, it was like a lifetime.

Just as the sun was starting to set on Friday evening, the boys made their way to Mrs. Milam's house. From all the experiences they had the last couple of years—more often than not, those experiences turned out different than they planed and most times, resulted in the *oops* side—they opted to show up at Mrs. Milam's house at dusk, instead of complete darkness. They did not want to run into something in the darkness they wished they hadn't.

Charlie and Jake walked across the street to the sidewalk, running in front of her house. They figured they could walk back and forth until she turned on the lights in the house, and then they would be able to see in while she wouldn't be able to see out. There was a large picture window in the front of the house on the left side of the porch. They planned to walk past the house one way about a half block, turn around, and walk back in the other direction. They did this several times until the streetlight in front of her house slowly started to come on. Once it was completely lit up, it was bright enough to light up Mrs. Milam's entire front porch as well as a little on both sides of her house. When this happened, Charlie and Jake walked back to where the other three were waiting. They were next to shrubbery that looked as if someone had trimmed it, trying to make it resemble a ball of some kind. However, they must of had no idea what they were doing as half of it looked square, while the other half looked kind of like a misshapen basketball with most of the air let out. All of the boys gathered together in the part of the scrub that was blocking out most of the glow coming from the streetlight.

"What now?" Jake asked to no one unparticular.

"Why don't a couple of us go on each side of the house and try to see inside. Who's to know? She might be setting in there on her couch or asleep in a chair," Bruce said.

"By the way, what are we looking for? Why are we even here?" Jake added.

"We are here doing our civic duty, checking up on Mrs. Milam. See if she is okay or if she might need help," Sonny answered.

"Looks to me if we were performing some kind of civic duty, the correct way to do it would be to walk up on the porch and knock on the door. When she answered, just ask her if she is doing okay," Gary said, looking from one of them to the other.

"Didn't I tell you my mother said she was meaner than a rabid dog? Who's to know when she came to answer the door if she might or might not be carrying one of them rolling pins or a skillet to knock the crap out of one or all of us for bothering her?" Sonny answered.

"True. That's sure true enough," Charlie answered.

So they decided to stick to the plan to creep on each side of her house. Jake, Charlie, and Bruce took the south side of the house, while Sonny and Gary ran across the street to the north side of the house.

"Gary, if we get caught by Mrs. Milam and she kills me for window-peeking on her, would you please tell my mother and grandmother that I wasn't peeking to see her naked old body or anything like that? That I was just doing my civic duty? That way, when I'm being buried, they won't think they were raising some kind of a pervert," Sonny whispered.

"Why are you asking me something like this?" Gary whispered back to Sonny as they leaned against Mrs. Milam's house.

"Because you can outrun me. So it just stands to reason I will be the one killed if there is a killing that is to be done, since you're the fastest," Sonny answered, smiling at him. "Boost me up so I can look inside the bathroom window."

"Okay, but you may be sorry," came Gary's answer.

"Why is that?"

"You remember Natty Sweepe before she died?"

"Sure, I do. Isn't she that the old woman who lived next door to you before she passed on to glory land?" Sonny asked.

"That's right. She lived all alone and never had any relatives. And very few friends ever stayed with her, much less visited her," Gary answered.

"What does Natty have to do with anything?" Sonny asked.

"My mother kind of felt sorry for her since no one ever seemed to go visit her. So a lot of times after supper, mother would make her a plate of whatever it was we had that night. Either she would take it over or she would get me to do it if she was busy. Well, one evening, she had me take her a bowl of just plain old okra. I have no clue why anyone would want just a bowl of okra. I guess as a person gets older, their taste buds don't taste as well, but plain okra? No way," Gary said.

"Anyway, there I was, big as Dallas, standing on her porch with that bowl of okra.

I knocked several time before I heard her call out for me to come on in. I went on in. She called for me to come on back to where she was. I wanted to just put the stuff on the counter by the sink, but I thought she must be already in bed and wanted to snack on that stupid okra while lying in bed. So I pushed her bedroom door open. I guess I pushed a little hard because it flew completely wide open and hit her cat's litter box. Apparently, when that door hit that litter box, her cat, Toffee, was in it and having herself a bowel movement. I think that I must have near scared that cat to death. I bet every time from that day on, old Natty had to give Toffee one of them cat laxatives to get her job done," Gary said.

"That's it? That's what I need to worry about?" Sonny asked, laughing.

"No, that's not the problem. I don't care if I gave some stupid cat constipation. The problem is, when that door flew open, there set Natty on one of them pee pots next to her bed, just as naked as a jaybird. She went to screaming like I was just some kind of your ornery pervert there to ravage her. I stood there for God knows how long, looking at her sitting on that darn pot. I guess I was in shock or paralyzed from seeing Natty setting on that jug all naked with everything just hanging out like it was. That view of her must have sent me into shock. I was so startled that I dropped that bowl of okra right where I stood. When my mind come to the realization what was going on, I ran out of there as if that old devil himself was about to grab hold of my shirt tail and drag me down to the pits of hell."

"Wow, that's not good," Sonny answered.

"Not good? Heck, I wasn't able to sleep for several days. Every time I closed my eyes, I would see Natty setting on that pot with her fat running off the sides of the thing. I'm pretty sure that this is about as tall as I will ever get because something like that can't help but stunt a fellow's growth," he answered, nodding his head up and down, trying to smile. "That's the reason I said you may be sorry if Mrs. Milam happens to be on the pot or just getting out of the shower. If you happen to see her like that, it will be a wonder you don't go blind. There is a darn good chance this is tall as you will ever get as well. We will be known around town as little people or midgets," he continued.

"Okay, I'll be careful and look away if that happens." Sonny laughed a little.

"I don't know how much time a fellow has to look away before his growth hormone gets stunt," Gary wondered.

Gary put his hands together to form a cradle. Sonny placed his right foot in Gary's hands, jumped up a little, and pulled himself up to see in the bathroom window. He looked in the darkened room for a second or two. Seeing nothing, he hopped back down.

"Nothing," he said to Gary.

About that time, Jake came around the corner of the house. He was half squatting while still trying his best to run. "We looked in all the windows around there. Nothing. She isn't anywhere to be seen," Jake said.

"Looks like we got to knock on the door after all. Let's just hope it doesn't make her gosh awful mad," Gary said, looking at the two other boys.

The boys walked up on the porch together. Charlie knocked on the doorframe several times. When they didn't get an answer, Charlie pulled the screen door open and knocked on the door itself. The second time he knocked on the door, it came open several inches by itself. Charlie had the look of a boy who just took the last piece of pie from the pan. The boys turned to make a run for it but Sonny whispered loud enough, telling all of them to wait.

"I think she is gone. We better get out of here before she shows up and kills every last one of us," Charlie said.

"Remember what those guys were talking about? They said if they didn't see Mrs.

Milam by the middle of the week, they would call the law to come check on her," Sonny said. "Well, we are here now. One of us needs to go in there to see if she is bad sick or worse," Sonny continued.

"Worse? By worse, you mean *dead*, don't you?" Jake asked.

"Yes, I guess that is what I mean."

"I don't know about the rest of you but I'm not in a real big hurry to go into someone's house without permission with a chance of running into a dead body. What if she's in there just waiting in a corner of the house with a ball bat and lying in wait, ready to clobber the first guy who comes within her reach?" Jake said.

"I'll go. I sure don't like the idea but I'll go," Charlie said.

"Let's all go. That way, if she is hiding and waiting for us, the five of us together might make her change her mind," Bruce said, looking from one to the other.

When the five of them pushed through the door, you would have thought they were all wearing the same pair of pants as they were so close together.

Charlie was in the middle of the group. "Would you guys give me a little room? It's hard for me to breathe."

"Good Lord! What the hell is that stink? Smells like roadkill or something,"

Gary said.

"How easy we forget. Don't you remember she was called the cat lady? I bet there is cat poop all through this house, making it smell like roadkill," Charlie answered.

"If that is true, then you would have thought a couple of them would have jumped out by now," Bruce answered. "Hey, just because someone is called a cat lady doesn't always mean they have a lot of cats."

"Don't know what else it could mean. I mean, the word *cat* pretty much gives it away," Gary said.

"It could mean she eats cats," Sonny said, trying to make light of the situation.

"Gross," Jake said.

As the boys, still all wadded up together, reached the bedroom, Charlie was just about ready to give the door a push when Jake said, "Hang on a second."

"What now?" Charlie groaned.

"What if she is lying in there in bed, all dead? You know, dead people swell up if they don't get themselves embalmed. She may be in there, all swelled up. When we open the door, the vibration might be just enough to make her blow plumb apart. Just how will we explain to everyone that we blew up Mrs. Milam?" Jake continued.

"Jake, you are a card-carrying nutcase. It's a pure wonder your folks would let you out without a keeper," Bruce said.

"You guys are my keepers," Jake answered, slapping Bruce on the shoulder.

Turning their attention back to the bedroom door, Charlie gave the door a little push. They were lucky her bedroom was on the front part of the house because some light from the street outside shone through the window. As the door slowly opened, it would have made no difference to the boys if she were standing right behind it because every eye in the bunch was closed. When they mustered up the courage to open their eyes, you could hear the *swoosh* of air come out of them, all at the same time. They saw nothing but a clean and tidy room. The bed looked as if no one had ever slept in it.

"Let's go. She is gone to visit someone or on vacation someplace," Jake said.

The boys seemed to relax somewhat as they turned headed for the door. Just as they were reaching the door, they heard a noise that seemed to be coming from under them.

"She's in the basement," Gary said as they all seemed to freeze in their tracks.

"Look here, guys. I've had enough of this Nancy Drew mystery crap. I'm ready to call it a night," Jake said.

"I'm with Jake," Gary said.

"That's my thought as well," Bruce said.

"Well, I'm going down there. She may be in real trouble, and someone has to check on her," Sonny said.

"I'll hang with you, Sonny," Charlie said.

Jake, Bruce, and Gary left the same way they came in, while Charlie and Sonny stood together, watching their buddies until they were completely out of sight.

"Okay, if we are going to do this, let's get it done," Sonny whispered to Charlie.

"I wonder how you get to the basement," Charlie wondered.

"All we can do is open doors until we find the one with the staircase leading down to it," Sonny answered.

Together, the boys opened all the doors until they found the correct one off the kitchen.

Standing by the door looking down into the dark basement, you could tell neither of the two boys was in too big of a hurry to walk down those stairs.

"Kind of know what those paratroopers must have felt like just before they had to jump out of their planes into the dark sky in the war," Charlie mused, still looking down into the dark basement. "Wonder where the light switch is."

"If it's like most basements, I bet it's in the middle of the room. You have to pull on a string or chain to get it to come on," Sonny answered.

"For God's sake, why do basement stairs always have to squeak?" Charlie grumbled as he started down the stairs.

"You got me by the yang-yang," Sonny answered.

"I guess it's just one of those things in life that just happens. Kind of like when a person uses the last little bit of toilet paper. They never replace it and they don't tell anyone. Fellow has to find out the hard way," Charlie answered, taking another step or two down.

"Let's hope we don't have to find something out the hard way when we get down there. Can you see anything?" Sonny asked.

"Nope, I can't see squat. Just feeling my way as I go," he answered. As his foot hit the concrete floor, he whispered back over his shoulder to Sonny, "Okay, we made it down. Just reach up as we move around. Hopefully, one of us will find the light cord. Good gosh almighty, it stinks down here! I don't know I can handle this for very long," Charlie said.

"Don't move. I hear something," Sonny whispered to Charlie.

Both boys froze in place, trying to pick up on the sound or sounds they were hearing.

"What you think it is?" Sonny asked, still reaching up in hopes of finding the string or chain hanging from the light.

"I have no clue but it seems to be coming from all over," Charlie said.

Just as Sonny was about to answer him, Charlie must have found the light chain because the lights came on all of a sudden. Sonny was just about to scream at Charlie for not warning him he found the light cord but before he could say a word, cats started jumping around the two boys. One cat landed on Sonny's back while another one jumped on his chest.

The same thing seemed to be happening to Charlie. Both boys let out bloodcurdling screams while the cats jumped all over them. Their eyes were trying to adjust to the bright light.

"My god, look at the cats! There must be hundreds of these things," Sonny screamed.

"Let's get the heck out of here!" Charlie screamed back.

Both boys started up the stairs as fast as they could move. Several cats were running in front of them; others were still jumping on the two boys. About halfway up the stairs, Charlie must have stepped on one of the cats' tails as it let out a piercing shriek. Sonny let out a scream of his own. Everything was happening to them so fast they couldn't comprehend the situation.

Once they reached the top of the stairs, neither boy had the wisdom to shut the basement door behind them. They ran out the front door, pushing it open so hard that it jammed the screen door against the far wall. Once they made their way into the middle of the street, they couldn't believe all the cats that came out of Mrs. Milam's house. Charlie figured there had to be at least a hundred of them. Sonny put the number at something like two hundred. Cats seemed to be running around at every direction. A couple of them ran up the light pole outside the house. Several ran north, some ran south, and a few just sat in the front yard. The two boys figured those cats must not have gotten it into their heads that they were free from the basement.

Hoping no one saw them, the boys headed to their separate homes. They prayed that the sheriff wouldn't be hunting them in the next day or so with a warrant for their arrest for cat-napping or breaking and entering in someone's home without their permission. When the boys met at the park the next morning, all the talk around town was where in the world did all the cats come from. Mr. Keck's golden retriever fell over dead in front of the post office. Everyone figured the dog died from either a heart attack or the stress of chasing so many of the cats running around town.

Mrs. Milam showed up in town a couple of days after this all happened. Several people thought for sure they were going to have to call the police on her with the way she went about accusing everyone she ran into of burglarizing her house. "Someone went into my home while I was in the Chickasha Hospital getting my kidney stones taken out of me. It's pretty much a shame when and old woman has them stones in her kidneys. Stones that I'm here to tell you felt as if they might be as big as golf balls. Then when she gets put in the hospital to get them things taken out so she can pee like any normal person and not have to pull the sink off the wall from the pain they are causing her while she is just trying to do her daily duty, then somebody has the gall to sneak into her own home, letting her cats out to have to fend for themselves," she told anyone who would stop long enough to listen to her.

"I am here to tell you one thing for sure, and that is iffin' I find that scoundrel, they best have their affairs in order 'cause I plan to put a world of hurt on them. I'll knock knots on their head or heads that it will take a week of Sundays for them to rub off," she threatened.

The boys never let it out that it was them. Mad as she was, they were sure that telling her that they were just doing their civic duty wouldn't be enough to not get those knots on their heads.

10

It gets hot in Oklahoma in the summer months. On those hotter days, the boys liked to head down to the Washita River to sit under a shade tree by the bank and do a little fishing. They really didn't care if they caught anything or not. Just sitting in the shade of an old tree with buddies and talking about whatever happened to be on their minds at the time was good enough for them. That was what they were up to one early July morning.

They were heading for the river to do some fishing, some talking, or just to see whatever adventure might happen to show up along the way, as it so often did. Bruce said his dad told him about a spot half a mile from where they usually went. He said that it was a well-known fishing hole used by several of the men from town. The boys decided to try to find the place as trying to locate it would be half the fun. Bruce said his dad told him to go to the first road just before the river bridge, take a right, walk about a quarter mile, and go through a gate. Then they should be able to see the trees that lined the river in the distance about half a mile away. They found the gate but the tree-lined river looked more like a mile away than a half mile. With nothing else to do that day, they all headed for the river after closing the old rusty gate.

"Someone should put a little oil on the hinges of that gate. It squeaks loud enough to wake the dead," Bruce said as he wrapped the wire back around the gate to keep it from swinging open.

They had to walk through an alfalfa field. The walking was easy until they got to the fence surrounding the field, where the grass, sunflowers, weeds, and small trees made the going kind of hard. Several times they would complain that they should have just gone to their regular place. Jake was leading the way when all of a sudden, he stopped and motioned for the rest of them to get down. Jake had a habit of doing stuff like this. They figured when he did it, it made him feel like Custer or Patton leading their troops. It gave him pleasure to stop the group so they let him have his fun. When the rest of the boys moved up beside Jake, they could see why he stopped them. It had nothing to do with trying to be Custer or any other general. Sitting, maybe seventy-five to a hundred feet in front of them, was an old black man wearing a pair of bib overalls with no shirt under it.

"What the heck is he doing?" Bruce whispered to no one in particular.

"I'm not sure what he is doing but I know who it is. That's Old Buster. You know, Buster Odell," Charlie said.

"That's right. I wonder what he is doing out here," Bruce said.

"I'm not real sure but here is a thought, maybe he lives in that house over yonder," Gary said, pointing at an old gray rundown-looking house. It looked like there was once a picket fence around it. The years and weather had long since gotten the best of it.

"You think he lives in that place?" Sonny asked.

"Stands to reason. He's here, the house is here," Jake answered.

"Look at the place. Fence only half there, weeds growing up in the yard. And I'm not sure but that looks like a chicken looking out of the screen door," Gary observed.

Before the boys could turn around and head back the way they just came from, Buster stood up and turned around to face the five boys lying in the tall weeds. "Boys, come on out. I done seen all you boys a coming this way, all the way back to where you opened that old squeaking gate."

The boys looked at one another with expressions of a person caught sticking his finger in a pie to see what kind of pie it was. Since all they were really up to was just trying to find a good fishing hole, they stood up. As soon as they all did, Buster motioned for them to come on over to where he was standing. Once the boys had all gathered around him, he asked them to sit around the little fire he had going. "What are you boys doing out on these parts?" Buster asked.

"Trying to find the fishing hole that Bruce's dad told him about," Charlie answered.

"Say, I know about that fishing hole. Been some mighty big fish brought out of that part of the river," Buster said. "In fact, no more than a month or so ago, I hooked me something from there. After I jerked and pulled on the critter for nearly half an hour, it done went and broke my line. Now, boys, I don't want you to get me wrong one little bit. It sure isn't in my nature to do any fibbing but I can sit right here and talk to you iffin' you were one of them angels the good Lord himself sends down here to earth to do his bidding. That old fish had to weigh as much or as near as much as one of them Chevy cars you see driving around town from time to time," he said, looking to each one of them.

The boys really didn't know what to say to that so they just all nodded their heads in the international sign of amazement.

"That your house, Buster?" Bruce asked for no apparent reason. Him asking something like that surprised the other boys.

"Yes, I know she isn't much to look at but it keeps the rain off me. Got myself a fireplace so it keeps me warm in the winter," he said, smiling. "I never was much of a fellow to keep house. My missus, she used to do that. But since she has been gone I just can't seem to get into it."

"How long has your missus been gone?" Sonny asked.

"Well, I don't rightly know since I don't have an up-to-date calendar. My calendar is about three years old but it has the same number of months and days. None of them seem to be in the right spot for this here year but I figure she has been gone near eleven days."

The boys looked at one another in surprise. Sonny said, "Wow, that hasn't been very long at all."

"Nope, not long at all. Anyways, if I wasn't ashamed, I would take you boys in the house. Show you just how bad a place can look after only eleven days," Buster said.

"Is she buried in Verden or is she buried someplace else in Oklahoma?" Charlie asked.

"I didn't place my missus in a graveyard," he answered, smiling at the boys.

The boys automatically started to look around. They were trying to see if Mrs. Odell's grave might be someplace around the house or worse, if they might have walked over it coming up to sit with Buster. They all knew about the worst thing a person could ever do was to walk on top of a grave. Walking on top of a grave could give a person bad luck for a solid year.

There was a story around town about Molly Gordon who went to the funeral of a friend. After the funeral, she walked around the graveyard looking at this headstone and that one, never once watching where she was stepping. On her way home, she ran into the back of the city police car. He wrote her a ticket for not paying attention to her driving. When Molly got home, she ran over her mailbox. Then walking up to her porch, she had a stroke. After she got out of the hospital, a person couldn't drag her to a graveyard. Sure, she would go to a friend's funeral but she cut it off there. She said that the next time she went to a graveyard, it would be because she was attending her own burial. When Molly's husband passed away from old age, she attended the funeral, cried, and went on something awful. But when they loaded his casket up for his last ride to the graveyard, she stood in front of the church and waved as if he was just heading off to work or on a hunting trip up in the mountains.

In one motion, Buster raised his hand in the air and brought it down, slapping his knee and letting out a big laugh. "Boys, they isn't no need to be looking around for my missus' grave. She isn't here or underground anywhere. My missus is in Jackson, Mississippi, attending her younger sister's wedding," he said, trying to stop laughing. "Her sister Audrey called me at the grain elevator where I work, told me she found a fellow that wanted to marry her, and if I would please tell her sister because she was sure my missus would want to be there for the wedding. Well, when I got home and told Deloris—my missus' name is Deloris—you would have thought she was getting ready for the rapture the way she started to throw things into a suitcase and made me hurry into town to get her a bus ticket to Oklahoma City so she could then catch a bus on to Jackson. You know, boys, I was mighty happy for Audrey finding a fellow 'cause I am here to tell you that Audrey was one nitwit when it came to brains. *Nitwit* might even be a little light describing her, maybe *imbecile* would fit in a bit better," Buster said, standing up shaking the pants legs of his bib overalls. "Darn old legs seem to stick to a body in this heat."

He sat back down and continued, "Audrey wasn't just a few stalks short of a bushel in the brains department, she was one ugly woman as well. I hate to say it about the poor woman but, boys, this is a pure fact. She had herself a job at the zoo up there in Jackson. They had to end up letting her go because most of the smaller animals was scared to death of the woman. They stopped eating completely. It was so bad that a lot of them wouldn't even come out when the people who paid good money came in to see them. I'll tell you just how simple she was. She heard the story of Jack and the Beanstalk on the radio one evening. It took her several days before she believed us that it was just a story. She thought everything that came over that radio had to be a pure fact. She slept with a long butcher knife, thinking that giant might be heading her way," he said, smiling at the boys. "So the good Lord himself had to be the very one who provided that fellow to marry her. I shudder to think what he must look like." He shuddered, just like he just got a chill in today's one-hundred-degree weather.

"What you cooking, Mr. Buster?" one of the boys asked.

"Just call me Buster," he said. "Well, boys, I'm cooking up myself some moonshine. I know there is a law against doing such a thing but since I'm not selling it and just making enough for myself, then I think the police will overlook it. But I would hope you boys wouldn't say anything about what I am doing out to my own place now, would you? And for keeping my still to yourselves, I'll show you the best fishing hole within a hundred miles around."

The boys had no problem with that at all so they all nodded their heads at the same time.

"Wow, this is the first still any of us have ever seen," Jake said.

"Well, boys, I am awful proud of this one. I have brewed my shine to be almost tasteless. And once a fellow has a drink or two, you can't smell it on their breath. It took me several years of adding this or taking this or that away but I got her done a year or so ago. You can add some of my shine in a cup of water, Coke, or tea or just 'bout anything and you can't even taste it. Well, in water, it gives it a tiny little sweet taste but that's about all. And what a wallop! Once a fellow has drank just a small sip of this shine, he would have a hard time recognizing his own wife iffin' she walked up to him and planted a big old—and, boys, I mean a big old—wet kiss on him right smack on his mouth," he said, getting up and shaking his pant leg again. "My shine is so strong, when a fellow takes a drink of it, it will darn near knock the wind out of him. The reason I made it that way is my missus would get mad as an old wet hen if she thought I had been taking a sip now and then. And when my missus gets mad, she won't cook, clean, or do any other things wife's are suppose to do for their husbands," he said, with a big old grin on his face.

While Buster was telling the boys how to get to the area of the river that was supposed to be the best fishing spot around, you could tell Sonny wasn't really into what the others were talking about. Gary glanced over at Sonny. He had seen this look on his friend's face a few times before. One time, it ended up getting Charlie's butt hanging over a fence next to a bull. Another time, when Sonny invited them to help him turn the water off for an old lady he had been helping that day, they were all scared near to death by what they thought was a vampire. So looking at Sonny deep in thought, Charlie figured he was coming up with another of his great ideas. He hoped this one would turn out better than some of the others ideas he got them involved in.

"Buster, what would a fellow like myself have to do to talk you out of one of them quart jars of that stuff?" Sonny asked.

"Let me tell you right off the bat, you are way too young to do any drinking. Why, no telling a jar of this shine might just do to a fellow your size," Buster answered Sonny.

"Well, it's not for me but I know a fellow who would more than love to have a jar of this. If I can get one from you, I will give it to him. He will never know who gave it to him or where it came from. It will be nothing more than our little surprise," Sonny assured him.

"Tell you what, I have enjoyed talking with you boys. If you will come back and visit some time and if you don't tell where you got it or anything about me, I will give you a jar. But if I find out you drank it, I will be fighting mad and you boys better not ever show up around here again to visit or fish. And that, my boys, is a pure fact," he said, not smiling at all.

Taking the jar from Buster, the boys decided to skip fishing. It was getting way too hot anyway. They figured they would just head on home and hang around one of their houses in the cool of the air conditioner.

"What you going to do with that booze?" Jake asked.

"It's not what *I* am going to do, but what *we* are going to do with it," Sonny answered.

"Well what?" Jake asked again.

"I was just thinking, wouldn't it be funny to see what would happen if we put some of this stuff in the water that the preacher and his helpers drank from?" Sonny asked.

"Are you talking about the tent revival the Baptists have been having the last three days?" Bruce asked.

"That's the one," Sonny answered.

"Isn't that where your grandmother goes to church?" Jake asked.

"Yes, but she really doesn't care that much for the preacher. She said every time her church has a revival, they bring in this guy to head it up. She said all he cares about is asking for donations and to make sure all the church ladies bring him enough chicken and potatoes to stuff his fat face," Sonny explained.

"Well, I know your granny, and she doesn't have a lot of good things to say very much about anyone," Charlie said, laughing and slapping Sonny on the back.

"That's true. She isn't that easy to get along with. But the truth is, she really is a nice old woman. She just likes to act tough."

"Yes, I know how nice and sweet she is. She must have hit me with that flyswatter a hundred times over the years, ever since I have been coming to see you," Charlie said, still laughing.

"That's true. She is a killer with the darn flyswatter," Sonny agreed.

"Well, let's do it. It should be lots of fun watching him," Gary said decidedly.

That evening, about an hour before the meeting started, Sonny and Gary made their way to the back of the tent while Gary watched out for anyone who might come around to see what they were up to. Sonny found the water cooler the preacher would be using. He spilled a lot of the water on the ground when he pulled the five-gallon jug of water up just a little and poured the moonshine in. He didn't figure that would be a problem though. As hot as it was, the water would dry up in no time. No one would be the wiser. The boys walked to the park to wait until the revival started. If anyone saw them sitting in the tent an hour before the services started, they would automatically think something was up. Once the boys heard the music playing, they made their way back to the tent. Each one took a seat in the folding chairs in the very back. Sonny could see his mother and grandmother about midway from the front. He hoped and prayed neither of them would turn around and see the boys sitting in the back.

"Boy, you and them hoodlums you hang around with need to get your butts in church. Stop running loose around town like a bunch of heathens," his grandmother must have said to him a hundred times or more. So if she were to catch him attending, it would be the same as if he walked up to her and said, "I'm here to cause trouble, Granny."

The preacher was already sitting on the stage off to the side while the choir sang several songs. Every once in awhile, the preacher or one of the attendants would get up and make their way to the side of the stage. They came back with large white paper cups full of what the boys figured was the water. During a break in the singing, the church's regular preacher, Reverend Good, stood up and introduced the man who would be giving the sermon that night.

"Ladies and gentlemen, I take it as a great privilege to introduce tonight's key speaker, Reverend Clarence Pack. Reverend Pack is one of the world's most noted authorities on major Bible events," Reverend Good said, as he waved toward Reverend Pack who was sitting off to his left. Reverend Pack seemed kind of oblivious as to what was going on around him. All he seemed to be interested in was to just stare into his cup of water.

The boys looked at one another trying to hide their smiles. They were sure that if someone were to see them smiling together, they just might know something was up. The boys did their best to act like they were interested in what was going on. They were interested, that's for sure; however, they weren't interested in Biblical events. They were more interested in the events that they hoped should soon take place.

After the choir sang its last song, Reverend Pack half walked half stumbled to the podium. People looked at one another. Seeing him stumble, they must have just figured one of his legs fell asleep.

"Howdy, you fine folks," the reverend started. "Yes, my fine folks, I am here tonight to talk about a few of the major events that took place in this Bible I have right here in my hand," he said, holding up his cup of water, thinking it was his Bible. "First, I would like to add my two cents about the great exodus of the Jews getting the hell out of Egypt. You people know back in those days, the Egyptians kept the Jews as slaves to do all their dirty work like build idols. They'd do most all the cooking for the Egyptians as well because it's a known fact that when it comes to making bagels and such, you can't beat a Jewish fellow. So the good Lord himself picked a fellow named Moses to get his folks out of Egypt." The Reverend tried to focus on the people sitting out in front of him. "Back in them days, Moses didn't have himself no radio. He couldn't buy a little advertising time to tell all the Jews to get ready to beat feet out of town. Nope, no radio at all. Hell, he didn't even have a megaphone to call out to them. So I am sure he had some of his buddies run around hollering, 'Okay, all you Jew boys and Jew girls, we got us an exodus going on here. So grab whatever the heck you want to take with you and let's get the hell out of dodge.'"

The reverend was still waving his Bible cup over his head. "Of course back then, I am sure no one over there in Egypt had a clue what he was talking about when he said *dodge*. They weren't any boats or planes that could cross over the great oceans to check things out in the early days of the Bible," he said.

Several of the congregation looked to one another, wondering what in the world was going on. *Was this a new way of preaching?* they wondered.

"That old pharaoh, Ramses, was one stubborn fellow. He couldn't let go of the idea of losing all his Jews because they were one hell of a bunch of good workers. A Jew could build one of them idols he made them build in a New York minute. Whereas, if he asked one of his own people to build an idol, they just had to bitch about having to work so hard. In them days, the unions had just barely gotten started," he said, spilling a little water out of his Bible cup that he was holding up over his head. "So the good Lord his very self got irritated. He consulted with Moses and they came up with the idea to throw some plagues on Ramses to get the old boy to come around. I won't go into all the plagues, 'cause anyone with half a mind should be able to figure them out, like water to blood, that's simple enough. Ramses wakes up in the morning and gets a glass of water out of the sink to take a couple of aspirins from all the wine he drank the day before. I guess the beer must have tasted like crap in those days so they drank bottle after bottle of wine. So that morning he gets a nice cool drink of water. Then around noon or so, still having the same headache, he goes back to the very same sink but this time, it is pure blood," Reverend Pack said. "He must have just about shit his pants seeing blood squirting out of both the hot and cold taps. I know if I saw something like that, it would have given me the squirts. It's too bad the Red Cross wasn't around in them days. They could have stocked up on their blood supply for many moons.

"Then, there came those darned old frogs. Apparently, there were frogs everywhere. Man couldn't go to the john to take a pee without stepping on several of them critters.

They was in the cabinet where Mrs. Ramses kept things, like her pancake mix, egg noodles, and the rest of her dried goods, stuff she didn't have to keep cold. You ladies out there know what I am talking about. It just pitiful them folks from Egypt didn't know how good a bunch of fried-up frog's legs tasted. They could have had a hell of a frog's leg fries. Wouldn't had to worry about the Jews getting any of them either because the Jewish folks don't eat stuff like frog's legs—those legs being unclean and all," he said, handing his empty cup to Reverend Good and asking for more water.

"Then along came those flies. The flies was so thick, most people wouldn't even talk to one another for fear of catching a mouthful of those little bastards. If any of you has ever been to a well-used outhouse that is a couple of years old on a hot summer day, then you know what I am talking about. Before you can get your pants down or pull your dress up to do your business, them dammed flies would swarm all over you. Now just think about being in that same outhouse with a thousand times as many flies. That's what them folks had to put up with. Them flies would have gotten all up in their butt crack something fearful. I bet there was just some of that constipation going on back then because who in hell wants a butt full of flies? You can bet none of them did so they just put crapping off, which gave them constipation like a big dog," he said, taking the cup of water from Reverend Good. "Next, I would like to tell you folks about boils. Yes, boils. The folks got plumb covered up with boils. Now, folks, there isn't anything that gets a sore on a person as a boil. You all have heard people say, 'Good gosh, I'm as sore as a boil!' Well, I am here to tell you that had to be where that saying first started. Yes, them Egyptians was covered with them things. If one of you would have happen to walk up on one of them boil-covered Egyptians, you would have thought for sure they all had one hell of a case of herpes or some kind of plague had overtaken the whole country. Them boils covered them something awful. I bet a lot of wedding had to be called off back then because no young fellow would want to marry a girl covered with boils. The only thing they could do on their honeymoon would be to rub boil cream on one another, and you can bet honeymoons are sure not meant for doing that kind of thing," he said, laughing out loud.

Some people were laughing. Others looked as if the man standing in front of them had gone plumb batshit crazy.

"Well, enough about the exodus. Led by Moses, when they got to the Red Sea, Ramses decided to send his army to bring all his Jewish workers back," he said, taking another drink. "There them poor folks were standing in front of that large body of water wondering, 'What in the hell are we going to do now?' I am sure several of them who were talking among themselves thought they were screwed like old Hogan's goat. But, being buddies with the good Lord, old Moses knew better. He climbed up on a big rock, took the stick he had with him, shook it at that body of water, and, all of a sudden, that water split plumb in the middle. There, standing right before all them folks, was a hole in the water that they could walk through to keep from getting an arrow up their butts by one of them Egyptians. Once they got on the other side of the sea, the Egyptians showed up and started after them through that very same old hole in the water. But once they was halfway through, the water closed back up on them, drowning mostly all of them. Those that didn't get drowned right off the bat and made their way to the top, them Jews chucked rocks at them and made them wish they had chosen something else to do that day other than chase Jews through a big old water hole," he said, taking a long drink of water.

Bruce and Gary had to get up and walk out of the revival, acting like they needed some fresh air. But, really they left to laugh out loud.

"Ho, folks, I am getting a little ahead of myself. I should have said something about Noah and his boat as he played a pretty big part in the Bible as well," he said. "You folks will have to forgive me tonight as I don't quite feel like myself." He wobbled on his feet. "Anyway, back in Noah's days, there was a heck of a lot of meanness going on around. A woman couldn't walk to the market alone in fear of being robbed or running square into a purse snatcher and such. They was also a lot of adultery going on as well. I'm told a fellow might go out to feed his goats—as they was lots of goats back then—but by the time he got back home, they might be as many as four or five men hanging around his house in hopes his wife might also be into adultery herself. I figure it is what is now called wife swapping.

Those folks were really into drinking and raising hell in those days. They really liked their wine. Most all the menfolk were winos. So there you have it, a bunch of winos, and AA hadn't yet got started. Along with adultery, wife swappers were hanging around doing nothing.

"So again the Lord himself got with Noah. Told him, 'Look here, Noah, we have a heck of a problem with all these winos and wife swappers going on around this area, so I need you to build a boat. Not just some boat you would use to go out trying to catch catfish, but a boat as big as an aircraft carrier.' Back then, Noah had no clue what an aircraft carrier was. Hell, Noah didn't even know one day a fellow would be able to catch an airplane and fly from Oklahoma City to Dallas in just a few minutes. But the good Lord being all-knowing, he told Noah about aircraft carriers, planes, and such. But he also told Noah to keep that under the rug. He didn't want that out yet to the general public," the preacher said, taking another long drink. "He told Noah that he was fixing to make it rain something awful for forty days and forty nights. So that boat he builds better be able to carry all the critters the earth has two by two because he was fixing to drown everything else around the area. Noah wondered if that meant birds as well because, birds could fly. If that was so, then his boat wouldn't have to be quite as big. But the good Lord informed him that flying around for forty days and nights in a thunderstorm was a hell of a bad idea. So Noah built a boat about the size of one of them aircraft carriers the good Lord just told him about," the preacher said.

"The people around the area thought Noah was some kind of a card-carrying nutcase. So, most days while Noah and his boys worked on the boat, the townsfolk sit around drinking wine and making fun of them," he continued, stopping only long enough to take a long swig out of this cup. "A fellow would have thought once those animals started to show up to board that boat, they would have gotten the idea that Noah might just have something when he talked about a flood coming." He slapped the podium with his free hand, making sure not to spill the water in his other hand. "You know, folks, it just isn't everyday you see a couple of lions walking together, not giving one flip about the people lined up along the road watching, or two bears, skunks, and such. 'Course, it would have tickled me pink if the two mosquitoes showed up and Noah had rolled up a newspaper and killed the hell out of them two bugs. After he killed them, he could have knocked the hell out of them two flies as well. Anyways, when the lightning and thunder started along with the rain, those folks forgot all about wife swapping, drinking wine, and such. Nope, those folks knew they were up that proverbial crap creek with no oar whatsoever," he said, taking another drink and stumbling back a little before regaining his balance.

The boys started to snicker. They figured it was okay to at least snicker at him as more than half the congregation was doing it. Their snickering fit right in with the rest of the folks.

"Those folks were screaming at Noah, crying for him to open up and let them in but Noah went up on deck and said a little prayer for them. If it had been me, I would have told them to lie down and lick their own butts because I wasn't about to open up and let any of their smart-asses on my boat," he said, snickering himself as he told it.

Preacher Good walked up to Reverend Pack and asked him if he was okay. Not smelling the shine on his breath, he let him go ahead with the sermon. He hoped that Pack would hurry up and get this over with before he caused the congregation to all fall out of their chairs laughing at him or get up and walk out.

"Now I have one more thing to talk about before I step away, and that is about a little fellow named David who took on a giant of a fellow named Goliath," he said, motioning for a chair to be brought to him. When a fellow pulled a chair up next to him, he used it as a prop to help him stand. Most everyone thought he was either having a heck of a stroke—and if they might need to call an ambulance from Chickasha—or he was plastered. Whatever it was, no one in the tent was about to leave. They wanted to see this thing to the end. This was the most excitement the town had since everyone thought a train ran over a woman and baby last year.

"Way back when this all happened, David was only a young fellow who herded goats, sheep, and such. There wasn't much else to do in them days for a young boy but herd critters. I believe all the jobs at the grocery stores must have been pretty hard to get in those days. Well, one day, he was sent to where the Philistines and the army of Israel were facing one another in a big valley. Now the Philistines had this big old boy. In fact, the book said he was a giant. He stood nine or ten feet tall. This fellow went by the name of Goliath," he said as he adjusted his weight on the chair. "About one or two o'clock every day, just like clockwork, he would show up hooting and howling at the Jews, trying to provoke a fight with one of them. No one in the Israeli camp wanted to face this fellow because they figured it would be plumb nuts for a normal man to run up against this brute." The reverend took another drink. He was getting very unsteady on his feet. If it hadn't been for the chair to balance him, he would have fallen flat on his face a time or two already.

"So there was David, walking around the camp and hunting his brothers when this Goliath fellow showed up whooping and hollering and screaming to the Jews up on the hill that they weren't anything but a bunch of sissies. He said that he would tie one arm behind his back if one of them would come fight him. Goliath screamed at the top of his voice for at least an hour or two," he told the crowd. "I am sure it pissed a bunch of Jews off but the Jews weren't stupid. They knew it would be suicide to take on this fellow so they just sat on those rocks on that hill and watched him trying to goad them into fighting," he said, starting to take a drink but spilling it before he could get it up to his mouth.

"David found one of his brothers and asked him what the heck was going on around there, letting this bully taunt them the way he was doing. I bet David asked his brother if he forgot about all the lectures his teachers had given on bullies in school," the reverend said. Everyone that ever talked to anyone drunk knew he was pie-eyed. "David, I am sure, got pissed the next day when Goliath started his trash talk again right on time. So he said something like, 'To hell with this crap. I'll run down there and show that old boy how the cow ate the cabbage.' With that, David hollered down to Goliath, saying something like, 'Don't get your panties in a wad, big fellow. I'll be right down there to put a case of whoop ass on you, you big ass bully you," the Reverend yelled, causing a few of the people watching him to fall out of their chairs laughing.

"David's brothers tried to stop him from going down to face the giant but David wouldn't have it. I am sure he thought someone has to take up for the Jews. So that afternoon, he scurried right down the hill to face the giant, Goliath. Goliath, not only being big, was a real smart-ass as well. Because when he saw how young David was, being only a boy, he really went into his bully song-and–dance, making fun of David," the Reverend said, turning his cup a little too much and spilling the spiked water before he realized what he was doing.

"'Boy, you mean they could only get a little squirt like you to come down here to face me? They must not think much of you. Why else would they send you down here to your death?' I bet he said something like that to David when he saw him." The preacher fell down into the chair. "I bet David answered him something like this while he was picking up a rock to use in his sling shot, 'Fellow, you going to talk me to death or you going to fight?' That would have pissed Goliath off something fearful so I am sure he grabbed his spear and chucked it at the lad. As David sidestepped the spear, he started swinging his slingshot above his head. When he thought it was the right time, he let the rock fly, striking Goliath right smack between the eyes, knocking the piss out of him. In fact, it knocked him smooth out. So David ran over to him, climbed on him, and literally beat the shit out of that old boy. Then he pulled Goliath's sword out and cut his head off. He held the head up so his buddies on the hill could see what he and God had done." Those were the last words Reverend Pack said as he fell out of his chair, rolled off the stage, and landed right into the lap of Reverend Good's wife.

That night, Sonny didn't say a word about being at the revival. In fact, he thought he was home, free and clear, when his grandmother and mother were sitting in the front room talking about it.

"Wonder what he was drinking," Sonny's mother asked his grandmother.

"Let's ask Sonny? Boy, you have any idea about that?" his grandmother asked, looking at him.

Most times, Sonny could read his grandmother's facial expression as she only had a few of them: happy, angry, and prying-into-someone's-business. Today, her face was expressionless or she might have an expression that he had never seen before. He hoped it wasn't that as she could know more than she was letting on, which was never good for him, or she was about ready to get into his mind, something she was really good at.

"Well, you know I have been giving that a great deal of thought. I figure he was one of them pocket alcoholics," Sonny answered, trying to show no emotion.

"What is a pocket alcoholic or what do you think one is?" his grandmother probed as his mother got up to do something in another room.

"To me, a pocket alcoholic is a fellow who everyone thinks is a teetotaler but he keeps a bottle in his pocket. That way, when he goes to the bathroom or someplace alone, he can pull that sucker out of his pocket and have himself a swig," he answered her.

"You think that is what happened at the revival, do you?" she asked.

For some reason, he knew that she knew he and his friends must have been at the revival, but he wasn't going to put out any more information than called for. She, like most parents, could seem to always decipher whatever it was a kid said.

"Must have been. I figure he must have taken a swig out of his pocket bottle just before the sermon. Apparently, he drank more then he thought. Then when he was on stage and the effects grabbed right smack a hold of him," Sonny reasoned.

"Well, that might be what happened. Still, there is one more possibility that could have happened. Someone could have spiked the water he was drinking," she suggested.

"I guess that could have happened but why would a person want to do something like that? Sounds kind of far-fetched to me."

"Boy, there are lots of people looking into this. I wonder what they will do with the culprits once they find them. If there is culprit, that is. I know if I had a hold of one of them, I think I would near beat that person to within an inch of his or her life for doing that to the reverend," she said.

"No kidding," he answered nonchalantly, heading outside before he let too much out and praying no one would ever figure out who was behind it.

His grandmother might not beat him within an inch of his life but she would make the next few years of his life nothing to look forward to.

11

One evening, a few days after the revival, Sonny was sitting on his porch with Charlie and talking about nothing special, like most boys do when just hanging around.

Mr. Finchmoore walked out on his front porch and when he saw Charlie and Sonny, he started hollering and waving his arms, asking them to come over. They had never seen him this excited before. The day they pulled the ghost prank on the other guys, he got pretty worked up, but nothing like this. Charlie and Sonny ran the thirty or forty feet over to Mr. Finchmoore's house, wondering what in the world would have him so worked up.

"Sit down, boys. Have I ever got something to tell the two of you?" he said, as he motioned to the two lawn chairs he had on the porch.

"Mr. Finchmoore, you better calm down. You're going to have yourself one of them heart attacks acting like this," Charlie said.

"If I had me a heart attack, I'm sure that would be the best thing going all around for me," he retorted.

"Why is that, Mr. Finch?" Sonny asked, knowing he was the only one around that could call him Finch.

"Well, boys, it's Janette. Janette Finchmoore. Janette is coming to Verden to spend a week or so with me. Please believe me, a week or two is way too long for her to be here. I got to figure a way to get her out of her as soon as possible," he said.

"Who is Janette?" Sonny asked. Mr. Finchmoore's excitement was starting to rub off on him.

"Janette. You bet I'll tell you who Janette is. She's my half-sister. Haven't seen her in several years. Thank the good Lord for that."

"You don't like her?" Charlie asked.

"Well, boys, it's not that I don't like the woman. I guess, if it comes down to liking or disliking, I don't really dislike Janette. I believe she is a good soul but she is nuts. Pure and simple, the woman is nuts," he answered, sitting down on the edge of the porch.

"What do you mean *nuts*?" Charlie asked.

"First off, she is my half-sister. I don't want you boys thinking everyone in the Finchmoore family is nuts. We got our share for sure but I wouldn't think any more than any other family," he said, smiling. "Anyways, when my mother and father got themselves that divorce, I guess Pa figured he needed a woman in his life to help with the cooking and such. My old dad wasn't much at doing household things like cooking and cleaning. He was just completely out of place anywhere inside a house. The kitchen was like a no-man's-land to him. I remember when I was around fifteen or sixteen, my Pa decided to can up a bunch of tomatoes that the lady next door gave him out of her garden. Like I said, he was like an alien that just arrived here in Oklahoma from Mars or one of those other planets out there a fellow can see after dark when it came to cooking. By the way, boys, did I ever tell you I ran into an alien several years ago from some far-off planet? Course, it might not really been an alien. Could very well have been one of them yeti."

"Yeti? What's a yeti?" Sonny asked.

"A yeti is a bigfoot. I guess yeti is the name the archeologist gave it. You know them archeologist got to give everything a name of their own, like wooly mammoth. You and I know a wooly mammoth isn't anything but a hairy elephant. If it were me, I would just call it a hairy elephant—nothing more, nothing less," he answered. "Anyways, I went down to the river with this girl. I thought if I could get her to walk down to the river with me, I might get myself one of them lucky kisses. Well, when we got down there, talking boy-girl stuff, I was fixing to plant a big old kiss on her when straight across the river from us, something started to shake the weeds. I figured it was a cow or someone's dog out sniffing around.

I believe we sat there for nearly an hour, watching the bushes moving first one way then the other. All of a sudden, this thing stood up looking at us. It looked like one of the gorillas they have in them cages up in the Oklahoma City Zoo," he said, looking first at Sonny then to Charlie. "But I am here to tell you that I have seen those gorillas close up and this thing looking at us was way taller than a gorilla. Sure, before you tell me gorillas hunch over when they walk. Well, hunch over or not, this sucker stood as straight up as I am right now," he said. He was standing as straight up as he could, to show the boys how tall it must have been. "And another thing, the darn thing had no gorilla face. It had the face of one of them prehistoric men you see in that national geography book. But we all know it wasn't a prehistoric fellow. No fellow from way back then would still be alive. It would have already run out of food several years ago," he said, sitting back down.

"Wow, I bet that just about scared the crap out of you two," Charlie said.

"You can bet it did. But we were more enthused as to what it was. She and I both stood there looking at it. It was like it had us hypnotized with its looks," he said. He started to sit back down, but he changed his mind and kept standing. "And you know what that fellow did then?" he asked.

"What?" both boys chimed in at the same time.

"That bigfoot thing or alien or whatever it was raised its arms and waved at us," he continued telling his story. "And that's not the worst of it. When it waved at us, it wasn't just a normal 'Hi, how are you?' wave. This thing shot us the finger while it was waving. Now don't that just about beat anything you ever heard before? So there you go. No bigfoot that I have ever heard of shoots people the finger. I told some of the men around town about what we saw. They just laughed it off, saying it had to be Clarence Thornburg, a hermit fellow that lived around that area of the river. But I'm here to tell you if it wasn't no bigfoot, it had to be an alien—an alien came here to check on us. I will take that with me to my grave.

Anyway, you know them aliens are really bad about coming down here to find out what us folks are up to. I figured they have nothing better to do on their own planet so coming down to earth to probe this fellow or that fellow is like a vacation for them alien fellows. Besides, I have seen Clarence several times in town, and this beast wasn't Clarence. Clarence would never shoot anyone the finger, that's a fact, and a bigfoot wouldn't know how to do that. So it had to be an alien come down here to probe a few of us because I sure don't figure one would fly all them billions and trillions of miles just to shoot a fellow and his girl then head back to wherever. Can you figure how much gasoline that would take?

"Anyway, I seem to be getting off track here," he said. "Back to my half-sister, Janette. Janette isn't your normal nut, like one of them normal crazy people you run into now and then. You know the type that will take cigarette butts out of ashtrays and eat them or those who talk to themselves all the time? Nope, she is a nut that's for sure, but not a normal one. You see, most of the time, Janette is just as normal as you or I am but for some strange reason, she will get crazy all of a sudden. We were at Jumping Jonny's seafood cabin in Anadarko having a nice catfish dinner one evening, just me and her and her fiancé, Bobby Green, when, all of a sudden, she jumped up, grabbed those little balls you get when you have fish, hush doggies or something like that—"

"Hush puppies. They are called hush puppies. I think they taste great. I could eat a ton of them things," Sonny interrupted.

"Okay, hush puppies. Anyways, she started to chuck them at different people sitting around. She hit one woman in the eye, another fellow in the back of the head. Most everyone jumped up from their seats and ran into the bar to get out of harm's way from those flying hush puppies. When she had thrown it all away, she sat down as pretty as you please and asked me to please pass the ketchup as if nothing had happened. Then she couldn't figure out why the owner asked us to leave. When she finely did marry Bobby, Bobby went to the bathroom on their honeymoon night, leaving her alone sitting on the bed, as the story goes. When Bobby came out, he was just as naked as the day he was born. For some reason, that sent her into one of her crazy spells." Mr. Finchmoore stepped off the porch and on to the lawn. "She went plumb crazy seeing her new husband standing there. She started hollering 'rape,' 'kidnapping,' and all sorts of things. The house detective rushed up to the honeymoon suite and threw the cuffs on Bobby. He was dragged to the police department and questioned for several hours before Janette came out of her nut spell and told them the truth. Needless to say, Bobby was waiting at his lawyer's office having the marriage annulled the very next day. He said he couldn't live with a woman like Janette, never knowing when she would flip out. Have him arrested, or worse, beat him to death with something out of the kitchen while he was sleeping. If not something from the kitchen, then with anything else she could find to put her hands on," he continued, laughing a little to himself.

"Now, let me finish what I was saying about my Pa canning those tomatoes before I say anymore about Janette. I seem to be getting to many stories going all at once," he said, sitting back down on the edge of the porch. "You would have thought he would put the tomatoes in a Crock-Pot to slow cook them like any normal human being. No, not my dad. He didn't do anything slow. So he chose a pressure cooker, filled that sucker plumb full of tomatoes, twisted the pot lid close, and turned the fire on under it. When the tomatoes started boiling in the pot, the little thing started to whistle like pressure cookers do. Dad must have thought it was broken and decided he better do something about that. He took a small hammer and beat the escape valve close. He said it was bad enough the thing leaking steam like it was, but he sure as heck couldn't put up with that whistling," Mr. Finchmoore said, shaking his head. "I tried to explain to him that it was normal for it to do that whistling. I tried to tell him that when mother used the cooker, it always did that and she didn't seem to mind. 'That's because women don't know one little bit about mechanical things,' was his only answer back to me. After only a few minutes, it looked to me as if the cooker was starting to shake a little. I knew for sure that wasn't supposed to happen. Again, I said something to my father about what the cooker was doing. 'Boy, stop bothering me about that darn pot. When it shakes like that, that just means the stuff inside is boiling like it should be,' was all he would say.

"I hope you boys don't think me a sissy or coward like one of them rats that runs from a ship is in trouble. However, I just figured if something was about to happened, then the best place for me would be as far away from that cooker as possible, so I walked—okay, I ran outside to get away from it. Well, it's a darn good thing I did because once I set foot on the grass in the front yard, I heard one gosh-awful big explosion. To me, it sounded like a bomb just went off right there in my own home. Fearing my dad got himself blown smooth up, I ran back inside thinking I would see pieces of him lying all around the kitchen.

Making my way into the kitchen, I saw a mess like none other I have never seen before or since. There were pieces of tomatoes or tomato juice all over everything. When the pot blew up, the bottom half of it hit the icebox door, knocking a big dent into it. The top half had blown a hole in the ceiling, landing in a big box of tax papers my dad stored up there. Dad was lying down under the kitchen table. I thought he was a goner the way he was covered with tomato juice and pieces of tomatoes stuck to most of his body. One shirtsleeve was blown completely off. It's a wonder the rest of his shirt wasn't blown off as well as many rips and holes it had in it. Then my dad sat up. The only thing he said was: 'Should never have tampered with that valve!'"

Finch was sitting back down on the porch. "And that, my boys, is how Janette came to be part of the family. He figured out we would more than likely starve to death if he didn't find a new wife to do the cooking. I guess I better get back to Janette before I end up telling you boys about everything but Janette. I received this telegram yesterday morning from her. Said she spent the night in Stillwater last night and would be arriving here sometime today."

"What can we do to help you?" Charlie asked.

"First off, you boys can come check on me now and then. If she flies into one of her nut stages, kills me or ties me up, then you can get me some help," he answered. "Also, Janette is scared to death of critters, like snakes, frogs, spiders, and such, so I got myself a plan to scare her with some of those. I will need for you boys to catch some of them for me."

As soon as he got out the words *catch some of them for me* out, a taxi pulled up in front of his house. "Good gosh almighty, that's got to be her. Good Lord, protect us, protect us one and all," he said, raising his arms up in the air praising the Lord.

When Janette stepped out of the cab, she looked like she could be anyone's grandmother to Charlie and Sonny. The only thing that set her off from other women her age was her blue hair. A lot of women in Verden had hair with a blue tint to it, but nothing like this woman. For several years, Sonny thought once a person hit fifty, some organ in their body kicked in, causing a blue tint to start showing up in their hair. Sonny's grandmother then told him that blue tint was put in at the beauty shop. She figured it was just to cover up all their gray hair. She explained that women hate the thought of getting old. Sonny found that out the hard way.

One afternoon, he was picking up a can of Garrett snuff when he ran into who he thought was one of Jake's two grandmothers. "Hi, what's Jake doing today?" he asked her.

"Jake? I'm sorry, I'm not sure who you are referring to?" she answered.

"Ho, I'm sorry. I thought you were one of my friend's grandmothers," Sonny apologized.

"Grandmother? Did you say *grandmother*? I'll have you know, young man, I am way too young to be anyone's grandmother, you little smart-ass you!" She was noticeably very angry.

Sonny got out of the store as fast as he could. He was afraid she was mad enough to hit him with a can of beans out of her cart or to start chucking apples at him since they were in produce section.

"Hi, brother," Janette said, walking up to where Mr. Finchmoore was standing by the porch. She gave him a big hug. You could tell Mr. Finchmoore wasn't really a hugger as he only patted her on the back while she squeezed him tightly. After she hugged her brother, she went back to the taxi, paid the driver, and took out two large suitcases. To the boys, it looked as if she had come to move in, not just to stay for a few days.

"Janette, these boys are friends of mine. The one wearing the striped shirt is Sonny, the other one is Charlie," he said, introducing the boys to her.

Once they had moved her things into the house, Mr. Finchmoore came back out and walked over to Sonny's front porch, where the two boys had moved, wanting to be out of the way. "Now do me a favor. If you find anything I might use to scare her now and then, please bring it to me on the sly," he said.

A few days after Janette arrived, Sonny caught a frog while the boys were fishing at the river. As soon as he got home, he gave it to Mr. Finchmoore. That evening, Sonny heard a bloodcurdling scream and what sounded like gunshots coming from his house. He ran over to Mr. Finchmoore's house, scared to death that she had caught him with that frog and shoot him. In just that short run to his place, Sonny wondered since he was the one who gave him that stupid frog if they could involve him in the murder. Just as he reached Mr. Finchmoore's porch, Mr. Finchmoore opened the front porch screen door and walked out to meet Sonny.

"What happened? Did you shoot her, Mr. Finchmoore?" Sonny asked in panic.

"Lord, no. Here, let's move off the porch so she can't hear us talking. Wouldn't do us good if she heard us," he answered Sonny. "That frog you gave me, I stuck it between the sheets of her bed. When she pulled the top sheet back and saw that frog, I guess it scared the pee-waddlin' soup out of the woman. She went to screaming like one of them banshees. I was reading the newspaper when she started to scream. Lord, it almost made me wet myself and I knew what would be happening. Lord, that woman has a set of lungs on her. But that's not the worst thing. She knew I had a loaded shotgun in the closet. She grabbed that shotgun, jerked around in the chamber, and shot that frog—not once, but twice. Not only did she blow the life out of the helpless frog, she blew parts of it all over the walls, not to mention, the hole she shot in my mattress and box springs. That woman has got to go before she kills me or some innocent person walking by the place.

"I'll tell you what I got to do. She has been talking about moving to Wichita Falls down at North Texas and taking a job at Sherman Air Force Base as a cook or something. So I've got me a little plan that just might put a little burr under her saddle to help her decide to move right on down to Texas. I have been thinking just how to go about that and I've come up with a pretty good, if not perfect, plan on how to do just that. Every other night, Janette takes a bath. So I need you or one of your friends to go to the river or anywhere else you might run into one of them old black bull snakes. Then when she is in the tub, you, Sonny, will put it in there with her," he said.

"Now how in the world would I go about doing something like that?" Sonny asked.

"For some reason, the PVC pipe that supplies water to the tub runs from the second floor down to the bathroom. Once she shuts the water off, the pipe goes empty. So if you were lying in wait and watching for her to shut the water off, then you could unscrew the cap off the clean out valve and put the snake in it. Then when she turns the tap on again to get more hot water, the snake should come out along with the water," he said, still smiling.

"You want me to hide up there watching, or should I say, peeping on your sister while she takes a bath? I don't think I can do that. What if she saw me? You said she went nuts on her honeymoon. Well, what in the world would the woman do, seeing me peeking down at her from the hole the pipe goes through? She is likely to go nuts, grab up that shotgun, and kill me, kill you, and half the town before the cops showed up," Sonny answered.

"The woman uses bubble bath so you won't be able to see anything, if you're worried about that," Mr. Finchmoore assured him.

"Well, I don't know much about women taking baths. Now that I think about it, I don't know one darn thing about women taking baths, and I really don't have me a desire to learn."

"Well, she will be using bubble bath soap so you won't be able to see anything that might embarrass you. The bubbles will be covering her up," he said to Sonny.

"Well, like I said, I don't know all that much about women and baths but it looks like to me, bubble bath or not, her boobs will be floating on top of the water."

"Boy, those things don't float. They aren't filled with air, you know," Mr.

Finchmoore said, laughing a little "Now how am I supposed to know that? I'm only fourteen. It's not like I have had been around the things all that much. All I know is what I have seen in the books at school," he reasoned.

After he stopped snickering at Sonny, Mr. Finchmoore asked, "Well, will you help?"

"Okay, I will help you but only because you helped me scare the crap out of the guys that time," Sonny answered.

It took the guys three days to find a bull snake. They ended up catching one that was trying to get eggs in Bruce's chicken house. They were not sure if it would work or not. They were afraid this snake might be a little too big to get into the pipe. It had to be all of four feet long. The night, it all came together. Mr. Finchmoore waved to Sonny, letting him know it was time.

Sonny very quietly made his way up the back stairs to the second floor. Once inside and finding the panel that led to the pipes, he went into the very confined space. There wasn't a lot of room for him or the gunnysack holding the bull snake. He found the cap over the pipe. He could hear water running through it so he knew she was still filling the tub. Looking down into the bathroom through the hole the pipe ran through, he could see Janette in the tub. Mr. Finchmoore was correct when he said the bubbles would cover her body, and he was thankful for that. He felt like one of those perverts his grandmother seemed to be always giving heck to when she was upset with someone or about someone.

"I tell you what, that fellow Don Dean is nothing but a pervert. I've seen Mr. Wallace at the store yesterday and he told me Don Dean was fixing to get married again. Fellow been married more times than I can count; now he is engaged to Helen Elders. Helen is no older than one of his daughters. Pervert, I tell you. He is nothing but a pervert. Someone should take that man to the woodshed and read him the riot act," his grandmother said one evening while they were watching *Sky King* on television.

Sonny was so nervous that if someone were to make a noise or if she would look up and saw him peeking down at her, he would wet his pants as sure as the sun would come up tomorrow. All of a sudden, something happened. He wasn't sure what it was. Then it came to him. The water had stopped running through the pipe. Looking down at Janette, he could see she had shut the water off using her foot to turn the white porcelain knobs. This was it. It was now or never. He slowly opened the gunnysack, grabbed the snake just under its head, opened the cap to the pipe, and started to feed the snake into it. The snake was so happy to get out of the sack as going into pipe was an avenue of escape. It went into the hole with no effort from Sonny at all. Once the snake was completely inside, Sonny screwed the cap back on. Then he waited and watched. He knew he should get out of there but wanting to see what was about to happen was too much for the boy. He just sat there as quite as a church mouse and watched Janette. He thought the woman had fallen asleep or died because she hadn't moved for such a long time. Then as he was about to leave, she said something. It was something he couldn't hear well enough to make out. However, he figured it had to be something about the water getting cold because she brought up her left leg and using only her foot and toes, she turned on the water. Then she laid back and closed her eyes to enjoy the warm water entering the tub once again.

Snakes are cold-blooded. When that bull snake came out of the faucet and landed in that water, it went half nuts, started jerking around, trying to climb over the edge of the tub, and falling back in after each try. Janette must have sensed something wasn't quite right. When she opened her eyes, the snake's head was about six inches from her face. If Sonny would live another hundred years, he would never be able to forget what he saw. She went to kicking her legs, slapping the water away from her and trying to get the snake away from her face, screaming all the time. Janette bounced out of that tub as if it were made of rubber. When her feet hit the floor, she was so weak in the knees from seeing that snake that her legs didn't seem to work. She reached up while still lying on the floor, trying to find the doorknob. Then she crawled out of the room, all the time, still screaming at the top of her lungs.

Sonny didn't care if he made any noise leaving the room because any noise he made would be completely covered up by her screaming. Making his way back to his own porch, he sat and waited to see what would happen next. Not hearing any gun shots for several minutes made him feel somewhat more at ease. He sure didn't want to be involved in a murder.

After what seemed like only a few minutes, a taxi pulled up in front of Mr. Finchmoore's house. Out came Janette, wearing only a pink robe and pulling a suitcase behind her. She screamed back toward her brother, "Just send the rest of my things to Texas. I won't spend another minute in this zoo, and you need not ever expect to see me here again."

Mr. Finchmoore stood in his front yard, waving good-bye to her. Once the taxi was out of sight, he bent over laughing. The rest of that evening, all the boys and Mr. Finchmoore sat around laughing at what transpired that day. As much as they looked for the snake, no one ever saw it again.

12

A couple of day before the Fourth of July, Chad Stevens stopped by to give Sonny's grandmother some eggs. Everyone in town knew that Mr. Stevens was sweet on Sonny's granny. He seemed to always show up with a couple of dozen eggs to give her. Mr. Stevens had more chickens than a fellow could count. He sold eggs to just about every family in town. If you bought eggs from the grocery store in Verden, you could just about bet they were from his chickens. However, he never charged Sonny's grandmother one penny for the eggs he gave her. He did, however, expect to sit at the kitchen table with her and share a pot of coffee.

"Wow, Granny! I think Mr. Stevens kind of likes you," Sonny said to her one afternoon, right after he left.

"Why, that old fart is nothing but an old pervert. I can't count the number of times I have walked by his place and saw him sitting on a bucket singing to those stupid chickens," she answered Sonny.

"Well, if you would let him sing to you, then he wouldn't have to sing to his chickens. Why were you walking by his house in the first place? His house is a couple of blocks out of the way to anything in town." Sonny smiled.

"Never mind why I walk where I walk or where I go. My goings here and there is my business and my business alone. If you don't want to feel the sting of my flyswatter, I would get off this subject if I were you," she warned him, getting a bit huffy.

"Granny, you try to hit me with that flyswatter no matter what anyways. Besides, I was only wondering if you might be a little sweet on him, too." Sonny snickered under his breath.

"Sweet on him? Good Lord, boy! I'm not sweet on any of these men in Verden. Most of them are perverted something awful. If not perverted, well, you can just about bet something is wrong with them some way or other. Take that old fool who runs that stupid produce truck up and down the streets, day in and day out. Most people thinks he hung the moon but I am here to tell you that if a man's brain was worth a hundred dollars, you would have a heck of a time getting more than seventy-five cents at the very most for his," his grandmother said, setting down at the kitchen table.

"You talking about Mr. Mayo? I think he is a nice guy. Several times he has given me and my friends an apple or orange off his truck."

"I bet you didn't know his mother, Millicent, was a witch, did you? When you were eating those apples and oranges?"

"A witch? You mean like a mean-old-woman witch or a person kind of like you when you have that stupid flyswatter in your hand?" Sonny was ready to jump away if she came after him for saying something like that about her.

"No, you smart little no-account. A witch."

"You are talking about a flying-on-a-broom-type witch, right?"

"Yes, a grab-my-broom-and-fly type," she answered. "I will say this for Mr. Mayo, he did at least one smart thing. When he got old enough to live on his own, he moved out of his mother's house. There isn't no telling what kind devilish things she has done in that house and probably still doing today, living up on that hill like she is. But only God his very self knows what that boy must have seen before he got away from his mother."

A witch. A for-real witch living right here in Verden, and this was the first I had ever heard about it. This had to be too good to be true. A real live witch walking among me and my buddies, he thought. "How do you know she is a witch, Granny? You sure it isn't just a rumor started by someone that just doesn't like the woman?" he asked.

"Boy, it's a pure fact. I don't know if I should tell you this or not but her husband disappeared under very strange circumstances." She motioned for him to sit down at the table with her as she started telling the story. "Her husband was a complete opposite of his wife. Whenever he showed up in town, he got along with most everyone. He would sit around with the other no-account men in town, play dominos, and talk about the weather. So, yes, he was a pretty good sort, I reckon;

whereas his wife, Millicent, was the complete opposite. It's my opinion, she would go out of her way to be a hateful sort. She was, I figure, the type of person who doesn't feel normal unless she was able to be mean to someone. Couple of years before you was born, the town was celebrating something or other. (Seems like every time something happens in America, we got to have some kind of a celebration about it.) In this case, I think they were celebrating some president who had died or didn't die. Something like that. Anyways, Bartholomew showed up in town. Bartholomew is Jerry's dad's name—and good Lord, don't ask me why any man or woman would ever think about naming their kid Bartholomew. It's way beyond my comprehension—"

"Who is Jerry?" Sonny interrupted.

"Boy, you need to do your best to stay up with this story. Who have we been talking about the last several minutes? Jerry. Jerry Mayo, the fellow that drives that darn produce truck around town," she answered. "Anyways, there sat Bartholomew with a couple of other fellows. Not sure of the name of one of them, but the other fellow sitting with Bartholomew was Wilburn Lee. Now, if there ever was a fellow that was a no-account, Wilburn Lee fit that bill to a tee." She stood up to get them glasses of lemonade. "Wilburn Lee never worked a day in his life, and that old fart lived to be something like eighty-five or eighty-six. He had one of them little oil pumpers on his land. It didn't make him a lot of money, just enough to pay his bills with a little extra to live on. He got himself married to Amy Lewis a few years after he graduated out of school. You can bet your last dollar that marriage only lasted a week or two after the wedding, just long enough for Wilburn to find out he was going to have to get himself a job. That little oil-pumping well for him just wasn't enough to support him and Amy, the way she ate. He wanted to stay married to the girl but he wanted her to keep living with her parents. She could come spend the weekends with him."

Granny sat back down at the table. "That just shows he was interested in one thing," she said, slapping the table as she laughed. He should have known that girl liked to eat before he asked her to get married. Any time anyone saw her, she had something in her hand to snack on. One time, I've seen her carrying a bag full of cookies, the next time, a slice of watermelon. And, believe it or not, I've seen Amy walking to the Post Office with a letter tucked under her arm, a turkey leg she was eating in her right hand, and a quart jar of what had to be brown gravy in the other hand. Amy would walk a little bit then stop to dip that turkey leg into the gravy, take a bite, and start walking again. She left a trail of gravy spots on the sidewalk all the way to the Post Office. So Wilburn had to know she ate like it was going smooth out of style in a day or two.

Well, those men sat there talking about this, and I suppose that was when Millicent showed up. She walked up to her husband and the two other men. She was so mad her face was as red as any fire engine you have ever laid you eyes on, boy. In fact, she was so mad she could hardly talk. Wilburn looked up at her and seeing how red her face was, being one to never let a chance to tease someone go by, he said to her, 'Cat get your tongue or did it burn off in your red-faced mouth?' He laughed out loud. When she was able to talk, she said, 'Bartholomew, you best get your lazy, no-account, worthless, husband-butt home because if you have the least bit idea what I will do, it won't be near enough.'

"Bartholomew didn't say one word back to his wife. I guess he figured it was better not to stir the pot. But those were not the same thoughts Wilburn had. As Bartholomew was getting up to leave, Wilburn said, 'Boy, she can't eat you. Just tell her to buzz off.' Millicent turned to look at Wilburn. If looks could kill, Wilburn would sure enough be on his way to Hanson's funeral home for his embalming. She bent down close to Wilburn to make sure he heard every word and said, 'Fellow, you best mind your own business iffin' you know what is best for your own self.' Then he answered right back, 'Millicent, you don't scare me one little bit. I'm not placing my boots under your bed at night and I thank the good Lord for that.' Then to the surprise to all the people standing around, listening at the two of them sparring back and forth, Millicent raised both of her arms into the air as if reaching for something in the sky. Then she whispered something under her breath. She said some words that no one around could understand. Then bending down and placing her face only a few inches from Wilburn's, she said, 'Wilburn, I hate to inform you that your life will be over soon. But don't worry, you won't suffer any pain.'" Sonny's grandmother took a large drink of her lemonade.

Hearing that, Sonny felt chills run through his body.

"Wilburn just smiled and waved her off as she turned to walk away, dragging Bartholomew with her. And you know what, boy? About ten or fifteen days after that, Wilburn was sitting around with some of the other sinners in town, drinking hard cider. On his way back home, he didn't see the express train when he started to cross the tracks. One thing for sure, she was absolutely correct when she said he wouldn't feel a thing. I'll give her this much, she was right as rain about that. When that train hit him, he was home with the Lord and the Lord's angels before that train could come to a complete stop. Most folks in town figured he thought he could beat the train but being so old, he couldn't move fast enough. Having all that hard cider in him didn't help him one little bit either.

After that happened, people got to talking around town. Most everyone thought Millicent had some kind of power to hypnotize regular folks. Boy, when a rumor starts up before it goes halfway around town, it will be stretched plumb out of proportion. And that is a pure fact. When her husband come up missing, the cops tried their best to locate Bartholomew. They searched every place they could think of searching. 'Bout two days into the search, someone told those cops that they seen him hanging around Mommy Linda's house in Anadarko," she said, looking serious.

"Is Mommy Linda's house a café or burger place?" Sonny asked.

"No, boy. Mommy Linda runs a house of ill repute. A cat house, if you have to know," she said. "So the cops run one of them raids on her place. You would have thought they were after John Dillinger or that Baby Face fellow from back in the '30s. The way I heard the story, they beat down the door with some kind of an iron pole. A couple of them jumped through the windows, while others ran out the back door. I'm told they nearly scared a couple of them girls to death. Several of them ran out of the place dressed in their birthday suits. Apparently, the newspaper must have gotten word of the raid because there was pictures in the next day paper or half naked girls running every which way. The headline read in big bold letters, 'Hookers Gone Wild, Running in the Streets'."

"Granny, I thought you said they were wearing their birthday suits," Sonny pointed out.

"That's a card-carrying fact, boy, but the newspaper put them little black marks over the girls' private parts. Wouldn't do to be showing naked pictures of girls in the paper. Might give a good God-fearing Christian man ideas to do some backsliding. Don't take much to cause a fellow to backslide these days, you know.

After all of that, Bartholomew wasn't no place around there. In fact, he hasn't been seen or heard of to this very day. But every year, old Millicent takes her prized pig to the state fair. Since the first day she started entering that pig in the 'fat pig contest'—or whatever you call it—that pig always won. People who have seen it says it's because it was the smartest pig living. They say it comes when she calls it and does just about everything she ever asks it to do: rolls over and fetches balls or sticks. It's just uncanny how smart that pig is. And you know what, boy? That pig's name is Bartholomew. Now, don't that give us pause?" she asked, scratching the back of her head.

"You telling me she changed her husband into a pig?" Sonny asked, laughing a little.

"No, I'm not going to come right out and say that. Lord knows that just isn't possible. But it sure give a fellow something to think about now, doesn't it?" she asked, getting up from the table to go about her routine.

Sonny was waiting to meet up with his friends to tell them the story. Once they were together, he relayed the story to them, not missing a word—except, he might not have told them about the black marks the paper placed over the girls' private parts.

"You say the witch still lives up on that hill?" Gary asked.

"That's right. That hill west of town, you know the one. You can see it from the school playground. Well, you can if you're on top of the slide. It's the big white house with all those trees around it," Sonny said. He told them what his grandmother said about the pig. He also said that his grandmother wouldn't come right out and say it, same as several of the folks around town, but they think she changed her husband into that pig. "After all, it has the same name as her missing husband," he concluded.

"Now I would be the first one to say I know nothing about witches but I got me a good hunch that changing a normal living fellow into a pig…well, it just can't be done," Jake said "Well, I don't know about you guys but I think we need to go up there and check that pig out," Bruce said.

It was almost impossible for the boys to not agree when it came to a prank, and this was even better because it was an adventure that might include a real live witch. They decided to meet that evening, make their way up to the witch's house, check if they could get close enough to the pig, and see whatever it was they thought they might see in her pig. None of them had ever had any dealings with a witch before. But it was like Charlie said, "When a full grown man is turned into a pig, it's not like it was done by the good Lord. It was done with black magic. And when a woman uses black magic, there has to be some telltale sign of the man still inside that critter."

They got close to Millicent's house a bit quicker than they had planned. If a fellow is fixing to go on a real live witch's property, he needs to take as few chances as possible. So going after dark was sure enough the correct way to enter her property, they figured. Charlie had wanted to sneak out his dad's pistol but after talking to the others, he figured a gun wouldn't have any effect on a witch. Besides, if his dad found out about him taking the gun, he would also be in need of the funeral director's services. There was an old vineyard about a quarter of a mile from her house.

The vineyard was the one Walter Young owned for a couple of years when he decided he was going quit being a farmer and become a great winemaker. Farming just wasn't making him enough money. Apparently, the wine he made was pretty good. It was good enough anyway that he decided not to sell it to the stores. Instead, he ended up putting all the wine he made in his barn. One day, he was celebrating the birth of his daughter, Ursula. This was something he did on October 10th every year for the past forty-seven years. Walter opened a barrel of wine, sat in the barn all day, and drank his fill. He drank so much of that wine that he tripped over something or other in the yard on his way back to the house and fell right into his well. Most everyone thought Walter drowned but the truth was that he was scared to death of falling so the doctors believe he died of a heart attack on his way down.

Once the sun started to fade a little bit from the sky, the boys made their way to Millicent's house. For cover, they stuck to the tall weeds that ran alongside the fence line.

"I'll properly spend the rest of the summer trying to pick tics off me from these weeds," Bruce whispered to whoever was within earshot.

"It's either get a tic or two on you or take the chance of being turned into a pig, just like Bartholomew was," Jake whispered back to Bruce.

"Bruce already had a little pig in him so it wouldn't be that hard to change him into one of them critters," Charlie teased.

"What? What the heck you talking about, Charlie? You hit your head or something?" Bruce asked.

"Seems every time I'm at your house, someone from your family calls you a pig. Yesterday, in fact, your mother said that you keep your room like a pig. Your sister calls you a pig all the time. So believing you have a little pig in you is really the only alternative I could come up with." Charlie smiled.

"Funny. Real funny. You're killing me with your wit, Charlie," Bruce said sarcastically.

R. J. Burroughs

When the boys reached Millicent's mailbox across the road from her house, they squatted down in the weeds to watch. They wanted to see if anything was going on and if she might have spotted them making their way to where they were hiding. She had her blinds down but they could see her shadow from the light as she moved around from room to room.

"Look, when she goes into what I guess is her bedroom in the back, let's all run to the barn," Jake suggested.

They only had to wait a few seconds before Millicent walked toward the back room. In the same instant, the boys all jumped up and ran across the dirt road to the east side of the barn, completely out of site of Millicent. They made their way through the side door into the barn. It was pretty much like any other barn. There were several bales of hay stacked up neatly. There was a large pen area that was closed off by wire. Inside were several chickens roosting on wooden poles strung across the top of the pen.

"Good Lord! Look at the chickens. If that isn't a dead giveaway that she is a witch, I don't know what else would be," Gary said.

"How's that, Gary?" Sonny whispered.

"Anytime you hear about witches brewing up some of their potions—love potions, potions to make people nuts or change them in something god-awful to look at—they always cut a chicken's throat. Then they smear the blood on whatever else it is they are using to conjure up their potions, like frog's legs, toenails, or hair from their victim," Gary said.

"You know, you're right, Gary. But here is another thought about these chickens. She might be keeping them here for eggs or to cook for supper. Can't hardly have chicken and dumplings or fried chicken without a chicken," Sonny said, slapping Gary on the arm and laughing at him.

"Look over here, guys," Bruce said. He waved his arm at the others, motioning for them to come over to where he stood. When the others got there, they looked through the small door in the back of the barn and saw several.

"Which one is Bartholomew?" someone asked. The boys' eyes were on the pigs so whoever asked the question name wasn't important to them.

"Have any of you ever seen a pig that was once a man?" Gary asked.

All the guys shook their heads no.

"Well then, it must be safe to say none of us would be able to pick out the man-pig," Charlie said to all of them.

They all laughed together. There were six or seven pigs in the pen but one stood out among all the rest. The boys had no idea how to judge the weight of a pig but the one standing alone by the far gate was way larger than any of the others. If Millicent's pig, Bartholomew, won the ribbon each year at the state fair, then this pig by the gate had to be her husband.

"Bartholomew. Bartholomew, come here, boy," Bruce whispered, just loud enough so only the pig and other boys could hear.

The pig didn't move toward them but to the boys, it sure looked like it recognized its name. It stopped rooting around and looked up at them.

"Bartholomew, come here, boy. Come over here right now, boy," Charlie called to it.

"Charlie, if that is really Bartholomew, then I wouldn't call him *boy*. Bartholomew...well, the real Bartholomew, is as old as your grandmother, if not older," Sonny said.

"Mr. Bartholomew, would you please come over here? We know who you really are. If there is anything we can do to help you, please let us know," Sonny said.

To the boys' surprise, he trotted straight to Sonny and started to snort or push on his leg.

"Look, he knows what Sonny said to him. It has to be him. It just has to be," Jakes said, getting excited along with the other boys in seeing what the pig had just done.

"Bartholomew, if that is really you inside this critter, would you try to let us know some way or the other so we can help you?" Bruce said, leaning down close to the pig's face.

No more than a second after Bruce said that to the pig, the boys heard Millicent hollering from what they figured was her front porch. "What the heck is all that commotion going on out there?" she screamed. "Bartholomew, if that is you acting up, I'll fix your wagon. Just you wait until I get my boots on." She went back into the house.

"Good Lord, she is going to catch us out here! We're all going to be pigs in a few minutes," Gary said.

"Come on, guys, in here," Charlie said, opening the gate to the chicken pen. He climbed through the little door the chickens used to get in and out of the coop. All five of the boys got into the coop just as they heard one of the other doors being opened. They sat as quiet as possible, not wanting to stir up the chickens and give away their hiding place.

Millicent didn't say anything to the pigs. She just stood by their pen, looking at them for a few minutes. Then she started looking around the area as if she knew or felt something was out of place. After what seemed like several minutes, Bruce bent down and peeked through the little opening just in time to see Millicent walking out the side door. She slammed it shut behind her.

"What next? Anyone have any bright ideas? If so, I would sure like to know what they are so I can get out from under these chickens. Something has hit me on the head a couple of times and I will just about bet any of you it's not raindrops," Jake said.

All the boys tried not to laugh but his statement was just too much for them. They all broke out in laughter.

"At least we know which is Bartholomew. But...but what to do with him?" Sonny said.

"Do you guys think we could do one of them exorcisms the preacher talked about in church a few Sundays ago?" Charlie asked.

"No, have you lost what little mind you have? An exorcism would never work. That is to drive out a demon or something like that. I think we need a séance, or something like a séance anyway," Bruce said.

"Yes, a séance might work but which one of you knows how to do a séance?"

Jake asked.

"Wait a minute. I think a séance is done when someone wants to get in touch with one of their family or friends who has died," Bruce said.

"You guys remember Amy Nolan? She had one of them séances to get in touch with her dead husband," Bruce continued.

"Why? What did she want to get in touch with him for?" Charlie asked, looking around at the others.

"Good gosh, how would I know what she wanted to talk to him about? Maybe she couldn't find a set of keys or she wondered if he ran into any family members up there yet?" Bruce continued.

"She might just want to find out if he made it up there or not." Sonny laughed.

"Say, isn't Choctaw Bill an Indian medicine man or something like that?" Bruce asked.

"That's right. If there was ever a person alive that could get Bartholomew out from inside that pig, Choctaw Bill would be the fellow to do it," Sonny added.

"That's right! Don't you guys remember the Scott girl? She was sicker than all get-out. All the doctors around couldn't figure what was wrong with her. I believe they thought she's nearly a goner. When the family brought her home to die in her own bed, Choctaw found out about the little girl. He made up some kind of a potion or something out of dirt, weeds, and things like that. Just as slick as a whistle, she was up playing with her dolls in a couple of days after taking his potion. In fact, she went back to school a day or two after that," Jake said.

"So what we need to do then is get Bartholomew out of this pen and get him to a safe place so Millicent won't be able to find him or us, as I sure don't want to become no pig, rooting around in an old mudhole all day long," Sonny said.

"Let's take him to Miller's old rundown barn. No one ever goes there but us, if you don't count a few pigeons now and then," Sonny said.

The boys found an old rope in the barn. When they figured all was clear, they pulled and pushed Bartholomew out of the pen and up the road. They went in the other direction from which they came so as not to pass by Millicent's house and take a chance of being seen. It was the consensus of the boys that if a witch caught you stealing one of her pigs—especially the one that used to be her husband—she wouldn't take to kindly of that. They figured if all she did to them was turn them into some kind of a barnyard animal, they would be getting off lucky.

While the boys pushed and pulled Bartholomew along the road, Charlie asked, "Say, what if we get Millicent's husband changed back into a fellow, you know, he will probably be mad as all get-out about being turned into a pig in the first place. What if finds Millicent and does her in? I hope you fellows realize it will be our fault for getting him out of this pig to do it. So all five of us will be in trouble for either him beating the heck out of her or worse," Charlie said.

"She is a witch. What part of that do you not understand? He wouldn't be able to hurt her. She would just change him back into a pig or a chicken or something. I figure he will more than happy just to leave town once he is out of this critter," Sonny answered.

It took them a lot longer to get the pig to the Miller's old rundown barn than they thought. They figured their folks would really be upset once they got home but at least they had Bartholomew in a nice safe place. They were sure no one would ever find him, or at least until Choctaw Bill had a shot at getting him back to his normal self.

The next morning, Millicent was in town early. The woman was near fit to be tied as mad as she was. "Someone has taken my Bartholomew. No, someone has *stolen* my Bartholomew," she shouted as she walked into the grocery store. "I have no idea who would steal an old woman's pig but I done called the law on them. And if the law doesn't catch the pig thief, you can just about bet your last dollar I will. And when I find the kidnappers, you can bet I won't go easy on him or her, whoever it may be." She continued to scream at the top of her lungs.

People really didn't believe she was a witch or, at least, some of them didn't believe it. However, no one talked to Millicent that day. Most of them wouldn't even make eye contact with her for fear what she might do.

"Have you boys gone pure nuts? That woman is a witch. There isn't no telling what she is capable of doing to you iffin' she finds out you boys stole her husband," Choctaw Bill said after the boys told him what they had done. "And now you want me to get right smack in the middle of this with you." He started pacing nervously in front of his house.

"You're the only one who has a chance of turning him back into a human, Bill. You're his only hope," Jake answered.

"Well, you boys need to know this is sure against my better judgment. I have never tangled with a witch. I have only heard stories from the elders about such things. I guess if I can help, I wouldn't be much of a man if I didn't at least try. I would be ashamed to hold my head up around my people," he answered. "I will gather up all the things I need and meet you boys at Miller's barn, say, around two o'clock. Then, I will give it a shot at least. See if I can help this fellow."

The boys all agreed to meet him at the barn at two.

"Be sure to sneak out a pair of your dad's pants and a shirt. When Bartholomew comes out of that pig or is changed back, I figure he will be as naked as a jaybird. Wouldn't do for him to show back up in town naked," Jake said.

When the boys got to the barn, Choctaw Bill was already there waiting on them. He was sitting on an old rusty-looking fifty-five gallon blue barrel that looked as if it had been used for target practice several times over the years. "You boys ready to do this?" he asked.

"Is there anything we can do to help you get him out of the pig?" Sonny asked.

"No, just bring him out here and tie him up, that's about all. But hurry because I want to get this over with. If anyone sees us doing this, they will send us all to the booby hatch, or worse, to the county jail." Choctaw Bill got up and placed the leather pack he had on the barrel.

The boys pushed and pulled the pig until they had it tied in front of Bill.

"Looks to me that if that Bartholomew fellow wanted to get out of this pig, he would at least move along a little better and stop putting up such a fuss," Charlie said.

Before Choctaw Bill started to do whatever he was going to do to the pig, he took a roll of duct tape out of his leather bag. Then he started to rap the tape around his right upper arm, from just below the shoulder, all the way down his forearm. After he had his arm taped up, he pulled a couple of leather pouches from the same bag. Then he took a little tin container out. When he had the tin open, he used his fingers to rub some red paint on several places on his face.

Watching him do this, the boys thought it must be some kind of war paint he needed to extract the man from the pig or turn the pig into a man, as it that was the case. The boys had no idea how this thing would work. Then Bill started to chant and dance around Bartholomew. Slowly at first, then as he danced, he started to pick up the speed. He reached inside one of the lather pouches he had tied to his belt and took out some powder. He threw that powder on to the pig and screamed something in a language the boys couldn't understand. They figured it had to be Choctaw talk. This dancing, chanting, and powder-throwing went on for several minutes. It was long enough that the five boys started to get a little bored with the goings-on.

Then all of a sudden, Choctaw Bill stopped dancing when he reached the back of pig Bartholomew. This took the boys by surprise as he hadn't done anything like this before. While on his knees, Choctaw Bill looked up into the clouds and screamed something in Choctaw. Then in one smooth fast motion, he spun his arm completely around in a one-hundred-and-eighty-degree circle. As his arm came around to where Bartholomew stood, he rammed his arm up the pigs butt in one swift motion. The pig went to squealing something awful, kicking its back legs and trying to dislodge whatever it was that just shot up its butt.

"Good Lord, would you look at that?" Charlie said, standing up while grabbing his own bottom.

"That's got to hurt," Sonny screamed so as to be heard over the squealing coming from the pig. "My mother gave me an enema a couple of years ago because she thought I had locked bowels or something. She used something smaller than a person's finger, and *that* hurt like hell."

As loud as the pig was squealing, the boys were afraid the people in town, about a mile and a half away, might hear it and come running to see what the problem was. They figured there would be absolutely no way to explain to anyone at all how Bartholomew got there. But even worse, how would they explain to anyone why Choctaw Bill had his arm up the pig's butt all the way up to his elbow?

Jerking his arm out of Bartholomew, Choctaw Bill said, "How I ever let you boys talk me into getting involved in this, I will never know. There isn't any man inside this critter. And I can assure you this pig is by no means, nor has it ever been, anything but a pig." He started to get the duct tape off his arm. Once Choctaw Bill had all his things gathered up, he informed the boys that they better not tell anyone he was ever involved in any of this. "Boys, if you ever tell anyone I was here, you think the witch will do you in? She wouldn't do half of things this mad Indian will do," he warned as he walked away.

Once the pig settled down, the boys walked it back toward its home. However, they let it go about a quarter of a mile before Millicent's house, hoping it would find its way home. They didn't want to take a chance of her finding out they had been involved in the pig-napping by taking it all the way home.

13

Two weeks before the boys had to return to school, Sonny and Jake were sitting on the front porch. Sonny's mother came out and asked if they would be interested in doing her a favor.

"Sure, what would you like us to do?" Jake answered even before Sonny could stop him.

"I would appreciate it if you boys would run a plate of food over to Mr. Henry's house. I drew his name at Sunday school and so I will be sending him his evening meal each night for a week," she answered as she headed back in the house.

"Do you just volunteer without finding anything out about what you might be getting yourself into?" Sonny asked Jake.

"What can it hurt? He only lives on First Street. What is that, all of two blocks away?" Jake asked.

"It's Mr. Henry. I guess he is a nice enough fellow but he will keep us there as long as he has enough wind in him to talk. I suppose since his wife died, there is no one that ever goes to see him," Sonny answered.

"Well, it's not like we were in the middle of a ball game or anything that just won't wait," Jake reasoned.

"Here you go, boys," Sonny's mother said. She opened the screen door and handed Jake the plate of food that she had placed in a paper sack.

Walking to Mr. Henry's house, Sonny started telling Jake what he knew about Roger Henry. "Mr. Henry is really a pretty nice man but can he ever talk. Every time I go there, he talks and talks as if he is dying in an hour or so and wants to get everything said before he departs this life," Sonny said, snickering a little.

"He doesn't have any family to come check on him now and then?" Jake asked.

"Yesterday, when I took the plate to him, he told me he had two daughters that lived in Chickasha but they had their own lives to live," Sonny answered.

"You telling me they can't drive the eight miles over here once in awhile to check on their own father?" Jake asked.

"I guess. When he was talking about them, I could tell it kind of bothered him," Sonny answered. "He said one of his daughters—I believe her name was Phyllis because he only said her name once or twice at most—is a lawyer. The other daughter's name is Gillian. I think he said she works at one of the drugstores in town."

Reaching Mr. Henry's house, they found him sitting on the porch and just taking in the sun.

"Hi, boys. What you guys up to today?" he asked.

"Mother sent you this," Sonny said as Jake held the sack out to him.

"Well, you thank your mother. Tell her, I really appreciate her doing this for me and also tell her she is a wonderful cook as well.

"I will," Sonny said.

Before the boys could head back to Sonny's house to get busy doing nothing, Jake turned and asked, "Mr. Henry, can we ask you a question?"

"What might that be?" Mr. Henry answered.

"We were just wondering why your daughters never come here from Chickasha, it being only eight miles," Jake answered.

Well, he did it; he had to ask that question, Sonny thought. He didn't say it out loud, however, but he thought, *My gosh! What is Jake doing? He volunteers like a marine for a dangerous mission. If not volunteering, he is as nosy as some old woman that peeks out her windows all day long in hopes of seeing something juicy she can talk about to other old ladies around town for a couple of days or until she happens to see something else juicy to take its place.*

"It's kind of a long story but if you boys will set down, I will do my best to explain it to you," he said.

Sonny wished he had brought himself a plate of food as well. He knew if Mr.

Henry was going to tell a story that it would keep him and Jake there forever. The boys sat up on the porch as Mr. Henry went into the house to save his plate of food for later.

"I guess you know we will be here until the cows come home," Sonny whispered to Jake.

Jake just turned and smiled at Sonny.

"Okay, boys, where should I start? Let me see," Mr. Henry said, as he sat down in one of the other chairs. "Phyllis, she lives in Chickasha, you know. Well, Phyllis is a lawyer so I am pretty sure she is busy all the time with her work. Anyways, it's her husband. He and I don't get along at all. In my opinion, he isn't worth a plug nickel. They had only been married six months when, for some reason, he thought I had lots of money put away. His name is Giles, and he thinks I am hiding money from him and my daughter. I guess he figured if I had really had money and gave some of it to them, it would make his life even easier than it is now, if that is possible. Boys, he is what people call a *househusband* or husband of the house, something like that. He lets his wife work and he takes care of the house. If you want my opinion on that, sounds like a pretty good gig. But I believe this entire problem between us started with the old outlaw, Belle Star."

"What? Belle Star? You meant that cowboy—I mean, cowgirl outlaw?" the two boys asked together.

"You see, boys, my grandfather was right friendly with Belle Star. He rode with her for a few years. The way he talked about her, it sounded to me like he was kind of sweet on her when he was drinking. But then, I was just a young fellow back in those days so I really wouldn't know if a person was sweet on someone or not," he said, bending over in his chair to get closer to the boys. "The story goes that Belle and four fellows—one of those being my grandfather—robbed a bank someplace down around the Texas Panhandle. When they were running from the bank, Belle got herself hit in the shoulder by a bullet. My grandfather helped her get on her horse while the other three lit out of there like someone done poured turpentine on their behinds. Well, old Belle and my grandfather, Miles Henry, hid out in a cabin for awhile until her wound healed up and she wouldn't have no problem riding her horse." Mr. Henry stood up for a second to stretch.

"I guess I should have told you, boys, right from the start that my grandfather Miles wasn't just a drinker, but a heavy drinker. Truth be known, he was drunk most all the time. Where most people carried food in their saddlebags, he carried whiskey. I figured he must have thought if he stayed drunk, he wouldn't care if he got hungry or not," he said, sitting back down. "Seems Belle was really thankful grandfather was with her when she got shot and helped to save her from the law so she started liking him as a boyfriend-type fellow. Well, all the time my grandfather spent tending to her wound, he ran smooth out of his whiskey. So being sober for the first time in a long time, he started to see Belle as a sober gent. One evening, Belle was so taken with my grandfather that she reached over and grabbed him by the bandana he wore around his neck and planted a kiss on his mouth, right then and there without a 'Watch out, here I come!' warning," Mr. Henry said, smiling.

"Why did cowboys wear them bandanas?" Jake asked.

"Search me. I guess, when they wanted to rob something or somebody, they would have it with them just in case they wanted to do some backsliding or something like that," he said. "Now, as I was saying, my grandfather was a drinker. Well, when Belle grabbed him up like that and kissed him, he near had a seizure from her kiss."

"Didn't he like girls?" Sonny asked, looking over at Jake and smiling.

"Sure, boy. In fact, a girl was his downfall—but that's another story for another time. However, being sober as a judge, he got a real good look at Belle. He said she had to be the ugliest human being the good Lord ever put on the face of this earth that he had ever laid his eyes on. He even went so far as to say he or someone had to blindfold her horse before she climbed on because if the horse caught a glimpse of her, it would bolt and run for the hills. She was so down-home homely, he said one older horse she was about to get on must have caught a glimpse of her and fell right over on the fellow holding it. Dead as dead can get. From what everyone around figured, must have been a horse heart attack. Anyway, Belle was so thankful my granddad saved her from the rope or prison that she gave him five bags of gold or gold dust since he didn't want to marry her.

"When my daughter married that fellow, Giles, it wasn't no time before she or someone who knew me told him about that gold I was suppose to have hidden. So he came out here one afternoon, demanding I sell it and give him and my daughter half of it. Said it would make his and her lives a heck of a lot easier for them to live," Mr. Henry said, sitting back down. "Well, boys, only thing I could do, since I didn't have no gold, was to go back in my house, grab my double-barreled shotgun, go back outside, and shoot above his head. When I did that, he took off running for dear life, thinking I was about to blow him apart with that gun. He ran so fast and hard, he left his car setting right there in my driveway," Mr. Henry said, pointing toward his driveway. "Anyways, it wasn't any time before he showed back up with my daughter and what I believe was about half, or more than half, of the Grady County sheriff's deputies in tow. All they did was to let him get in his car and head back to Chickasha with the deputies still in tow. To this day, I wonder how long it took him to find the two fish I put under his seat." He smiled at the memory.

"You put some dead fish under his car seat?" Jack laughed.

"I only did that to give them the fish for their supper. It was the least I could do with him coming over to visit and all," he answered, still laughing. "My other daughter's name is Gillian. Her husband's name is Burgess. Talk about a loser. If there ever was a loser, it has to be Burgess. Wouldn't surprise me one iota if he didn't graduate from the school of losers with honors. When he and Gillian first got themselves married, they were going to honeymoon in Las Vegas for a few days, then come back to put money down on a house they had picked out a couple months before they hitched up. Anyways, when they got to Vegas, Burgess got himself hooked on gambling. They drove to Vegas in a right nice car but came back on a really nice airplane. Now, don't that make a girl's father proud of the man she chose to marry?" he asked.

"Now, I am told he goes out with other women. In other words, the man is a cheater. To me, there isn't much lower than someone who would cheat on his wife or husband. But that is something that fellow will have to take up with the Lord himself.

What really blows a person's dress up is that my daughter puts up with that nonsense and my daughter would rather put up with this fellow than send him packing or come stay with me," he continued. "So, boys, now all my life seems to be an old man living off his social security, getting plates of food from the church ladies, and waiting and watching for the day the good Lord decides to call him home," he said, looking a little sad for the first time that day.

"It hasn't always been this way, boys. Did you know that at one time, I was a police officer in Anadarko? In fact, I was the youngest and smallest cop that ever was, or I guess, will ever be, since they put weight limits on new recruits. Back then, a fellow didn't get much training. All I had to do before I could start work was to wait until I could obtain a uniform altered to fit me. All the uniforms the town had were way too large," he said, laughing out loud. "Took about ten days before I could have me one made up. But as soon as I did, they let me have my own cop car and sent me out to keep law and order.

Boys, you couldn't count the number of times folks would call the station when they saw me driving around in one of the patrol cars. They thought some kid had stolen one of the patrol cars.

"My very first call was a suicide. This fellow, I guess, was all fed up with the world and such. His wife always nagging about this or that. So he takes a pistol and shoots himself right smack in the left side of his head. When I got there, it was one gosh-awful looking mess. I am here to tell you, if I hadn't worked in a funeral home when I was in high school, I don't know if I could have taken it. Anyway, after they loaded that fellow up in the ambulance and drove away, the chief of police pulls up with the chief of detectives. When they walked up to me, they asked in front of all the family members that had gathered around, 'Officer Henry, how did he look?' I said, 'Well, he looked dead.' When the family heard me say that, they went to screaming and crying like all get-out. Wasn't but a short time after I got back in my patrol car before I was called to the station and told to never say 'He looked dead' again. That I should say 'He looked critical' or 'He looked bad.' I told the chiefs that I worked at a funeral home when I was in school, and I knew dead. That man was dead," he said, laughing out loud.

"My next call was to a biker bar downtown. Word came over the radio that there had been a stabbing there so I headed right down to the bar. No one told me I was to wait on other officers for help, the place being such a known bad spot. So when I get there, the place is packed with these biker types, all big burley fellows with not one smile among the bunch, even if Bob Hope his very self was standing among those fellows telling jokes. I tried my very best to get by them but they wouldn't get out of my way. I feared that the fellow who got himself stabbed might be lying back there somewhere bleeding, like some old hog at the slaughterhouse. I figured the only thing I could do in that situation was to go back to my patrol car and grab my shotgun. When I did that, I walked back in that bar and fired off a round into the ceiling. Boys, the bikers split as if the United States Marines had just landed. Just bigger than Dallas, I was called to the station yet again and told never to fire my gun again like that. I told the captain I thought a man was dying. Course, we found out later it was a prank call. So when the desk job came open, I got stuck to take calls and dispatch other officers. After about a year of that, I quit," he said.

On the way home, the boys made a mental note to stop by and see Mr. Henry now and then so he wouldn't feel so alone. Besides, he told great stories. And there was nothing better than a good story by a long shot.

14

One Saturday morning, the boys stopped by Sonny's house. Charlie had some news that all of the boys were excited to hear.

"My dad asked me if I would walk out to Uncle Billy Bob's to see how he is doing. I guess he is a little worried about him since he hasn't been in town in such a long time. And my dad has tried to call him several times with no answer," Charlie said.

"Great, when are we leaving?" Bruce asked with noticeable excitement in his voice.

The other boys had excitement running through them as well. Charlie's Uncle Billy Bob was in the navy during World War II. He was stationed on the carrier USS Enterprise, and after all the action he saw in the South Pacific, he was never quite right. It was as if he had gone nuts from the strain. The doctors thought he was addicted to adrenalin because he just didn't feel normal unless something exciting was happening in his life to get that adrenalin pumping. If he didn't have something exciting going on, he just seemed to mope around until something happened to get the adrenalin pumping again. His favorite trick to get a little excitement going in his life was to put a blindfold on then toss a couple of butcher knives up in the air. Then he would move around in hopes that when they came back down, neither of the two would hit him. That worked a few times but after a while, it just didn't seem very exciting for him anymore. So he added a knife, then another, until he was tossing up seven knives. Then one afternoon, one of the knives came down and nearly cut off his left ear. That was the last time he tried that little trick.

Next he tried car and truck jumping. Billy Bob lived about a mile down a dirt road and he could see the dust from the cars coming long before they got there. He would hide behind a large scrub in his front yard and when the car or truck was close enough, he would run across the road in front of it, hoping not to be hit. The closer the car's bumper came to hitting him, the better. Soon the word was out about Billy Bob and his car jumping, so several of the boys in town would drive by trying to hit him for spite. This went on for several years. When Billy Bob was feeling down, he would run out and hide behind that scrub until a car or truck came by, then out he would pop again. One day, he didn't judge the speed of a corvette correctly and got himself knocked into the far ditch with a broken pelvis. That kept him in the Anadarko hospital for three months.

After that, he decided to give up car jumping as well. He still did things most people would consider eccentric, or as some people put it, downright weird. However, to the boys, it was more than exciting going out to his place as they never knew what might be happening.

When the boys reached Billy Bob's house, he was sitting on top of an old bathtub that was turned upside down. He was leaning back against a pile of wooden crates, eating a sandwich, and holding a pop between his legs.

"What brings you boys out this way?" he asked, looking from one of them to the other.

"Dad was worried about you, Uncle Billy. Wanted me to come out and check on you," Charlie answered.

"Your dad is a worrier when they is no need one little bit to do so. Heck, he would worry about being hanged if they was going to use a gold rope to do it," he said, smiling.

Just as Charlie was about to ask him something else, a man walked out of the house and sat down on the porch swing.

"Who is that, Uncle Billy?" Charlie asked.

"Ho, that's Jordan something or other. I met him a week or so ago in Chickasha. He was on the corner with a sign that read 'I will work for food.' So my needing lots of work done around the place, I brought him out here to do the odd jobs around my house. And the good thing about it, he don't eat much at all. But give him a bottle of hooch and he will have that drank up in no more than three drinks," Billy Bob explained.

Before Charlie could open his mouth to say one thing about what Billy just told him, another man walked out and sat in the swing with Jordan.

"Good Lord, who is that other guy?' Charlie asked.

"That's Clarence. Remember Jordan? The guy who will work for food? That is his brother, Clarence. Course, they must have had different mothers or fathers because to me, Clarence looks to have a little Mexican in him, whereas Jordan there is as black as a moonless night. But Clarence and Jordan are right friendly fellows, and there isn't a dirty dish anywhere in my house. When old Clarence isn't drunk, he is a cleaning fool. That old boy could hold his own against one of those Kirby sweepers that someone or other is always trying to sell me. Fact is, I had me a Kirby salesman out here no more than three or four days ago, trying to talk me into buying one of them vacuums. I just told him I had no need for one. I had me a fellow that cleaned like it was going out of style," he said, looking from one boy to the other.

Just as Billy finished telling the boys about the salesman, out walked an older woman with a pot of what the boys figured was water. She tossed the water out on the yard, turned, and went back into the house. None of the boys had time to ask Billy who she was before he spoke up about her himself.

"Boys, that is Lillie May Valentine. I know she isn't much to look at but can that woman ever cook. She used to be a Mennonite but her being kind of homely, all of the Mennonite men apparently didn't want to have anything at all to do with her. So I guess she jumped ship from the Mennonites to get herself out in the world to find herself a fellow. You know, I believe she is still a full-blooded Mennonite, even if she quit those folks. She still wanted to have herself a mess of babies, however. One thing a fellow can say about Mennonites is that they like having babies, and Lord can they ever cook. Boys, she has only been here a couple of weeks and I have already put on three or four pounds," he said, smiling while patting himself on his stomach.

"Well, what is she doing here? Lord, Uncle Billy, you didn't kidnap that lady did you?" Charlie asked.

"No, no. She was cooking at a café in Anadarko. Apparently, the owner made her give him half of her tips, and you know cooks don't get all that many tips anyway. But apparently, every time someone would lay a dollar or two down for the cook, he would take half of it so she just up and quit. I found her living in the park, cooking pancakes over an open fire one morning while she checked out the men who walked by. She invited me to eat with her, and me being a tad hungry, I accepted. Boys, after I put one of those cakes in my mouth, I knew I needed her to come out here and cook for us. So right then and there, as soon as I had finished eating, I asked her if she would like to move out to my place in Verden and do a little cooking for us.

She said she was tired of the park. Said she would do it but she also wanted to make it clear that as soon as she met up with a fellow to marry, she would be out of here. Also, there would be absolutely no hanky-panky whatsoever," he said, smiling. "But I sure don't want you guys to get the wrong idea either. She has her own room out back. All she does is cook then walk to town after to check out any new men prospects she might have missed last time she was checking them out. And, like I said, she isn't that much of a looker so none of us bother her."

"Uncle Billy, you don't know anything about these people. They could murder you in your sleep at night," Charlie pointed out.

"Yes, isn't that the truth? Makes a man keep on his toes, wondering which one of these three would do me in. Heck, it keeps my excitement perking all day and night," he said, smiling. "With them here, I have plenty to think about, which keeps me from tossing knifes or dodging cars."

Jordan walked out to where they were all talking. "How are you boys doing or should I say, getting along?" he asked.

"Jordan, this here boy in the white T-shirt is my nephew. The other boys are his friends and mine. They just come out to visit me," Billy Bob explained. "Why don't you give them a little bit of your wisdom while I run into the house for a minute or two."

As Billy walked back toward the house, Jordan said, "Well, boys, I know I don't look like much right now. The fact is, I guess I look like a bum. But now that I think about it, I am a bum," he said, laughing.

"I bet that's a hard life, never knowing where you will sleep or when you might eat," Jake said.

"Yes, it is something a person has to be either in a bind or just wants to give up on society altogether to get into this type of life," he admitted. "Being a black man doesn't make it any easier either. Course, boys, I haven't always been a bum. To tell the truth, the word *bum* is kind of a hateful word. I think it means something like an irresponsible or worthless person so I don't use it when I refer to my friends because I don't think anyone is worthless. Sure, I am here cleaning and doing odd jobs for meals, and I am appreciative of the job. I was darn sure glad when Billy offered it to me," he said.

"I don't want to sound callous, but is this all you have ever done?" Gary asked.

"Boys, you may not believe this, but I use to be a preacher. But got my fill of that after doing it for twenty-seven years," he said, laughing. "Please, boys, don't get me wrong, I am still a God-fearing man. I believe in the hereafter just as much as I did the day I gave my life to becoming a preacher. It's the folks I had to put up with. I hate to say it, but church folks are some of the most gosh-awful folks the good Lord put on the face of this earth. For instance, take Gertrude Mabel Scroggins, a lady who was in my congregation. Whenever the doors to the church were open, Gertrude was someplace inside. You could just about bet your last dollar on it. If that old bitty wasn't singing off-key during church, she was complaining about something. One Sunday morning she came to me complaining about Susanna Hester and Bucky Dennis sitting so close together. She said I sure needed to do something about them two kids. That if the Lord himself was to come floating down next to the pulpit, Bucky Dennis wouldn't have no clue because he couldn't concentrate on anything but that girl, wearing the short dresses like she does. She was downright afraid this might lead to a case of adultery.

I tried to explain to the old bitty there wasn't much chance for adultery right then, seeing the kids were still in kindergarten. Wasn't but a day or two after that she came to me, telling me that during the night—she figured around 1:00 a.m. because around one is when nature calls her each night—an angel named Bernard showed up in her bedroom. Said it scared her near to death. If she hadn't been wearing one of them adult diapers, she would have had to buy a new mattress. Once she figured out that Bernard the angel was just that, an angel, she said calm overtook her like something she had never known before.

Gertrude said she wasn't completely sure but she thought she was floating all the time Bernard was relaying a message to her from the Almighty his very self. She said he told her that the good Lord sure enjoyed the singing from the church choir but he wasn't pleased with the choir robes they wore at all. He wanted her to bring the matter up to me as soon as possible," Jordan said, laughing. "Boys, you would be surprised the number of times someone came to me, telling me the Lord touched their hearts with a message. Now don't get me wrong, I know for a fact the Lord does speak to people. I just don't think the Lord speaks to people as much as they think," he said.

You could tell the boys were enjoying Jordan's stories. Apparently, he had a very enjoyable way of expressing himself.

"Had a fellow come to me once right after church services. Said the good Lord touched his heart just as the collection plate was being passed around. Said the Lord told him he needed to divorce his wife, Bridget, as soon as possible. Said the Lord told him Bridget had been having perverted thoughts about the assistant principal at the junior high school. I tried to explain to him that the Lord hated divorce, that he would never advise anyone to divorce. But, the fellow wouldn't go for that. In fact, I read in the paper a couple of days later that he had filed for divorce. And you know what really takes the cake, boys? Wasn't but a week or two later I saw his name in the paper that he had filed for a marriage license with Patience Ball, a girl who worked at the junior high school, of all places. Then about two weeks after that, I read where he had been run over and killed by Bridget, his ex-wife. Apparently, Bridget didn't get the word the Lord himself had started all this," he said, still laughing.

"Then you have these folks who want you to pray for them—which is a good thing if they have cancer or some dreaded thing happening to them—or pray for a loved one. But not so that Isaac can have a winning night at the track or for this team to beat that team. As far as I know, the Lord doesn't take sides in sporting events," he said. "Boys, I was setting in a coffee shop one morning, having a cup of coffee and looking the newspaper over, when this young girl came over to me and asked if she could please sit down because she had a question. Being a preacher, I said yes. Sitting down, she told me her name was Esther Tucker. Then she leaned over and whispered to me that she wanted to have a baby.

I sure had no clue what in the world she was giving me that information for. If she wanted a baby or didn't, it was no business of the church's, much less mine. I explained this to the young girl. She said, 'No, no, you don't understand what I am talking about. I have to have your help or I will never be able to have a child. I know why I haven't been able to conceive a child yet. It's my husband.' Then leaning over closer to me, she whispered, 'You see, I believe it's his ding-a-ling.' 'His what?' I asked the woman. 'It's his ding-a-ling. You see, I think it's way too small. So if you would ask God tonight to stretch his ding-a-ling, I think that should do the trick. Tell the Lord he doesn't have to stretch it a lot, say three or four inches should do the trick.' I told the girl I would pray for her. However, when I said my payers that night the word *ding-a-ling* was not used. I did ask him to help the lady conceive but that was as far as I went with that request."

"People really ask for things like that?" Bruce asked.

"You bet they do. Had one fellow ask me to ask God to please fix it when his wife passed gas that the smell wouldn't be so bad. He didn't mind her passing gas so much, but the smell was so bad that he was thinking about building an extra room on his house for her to sleep in. Yes, people can come up with some really crazy things," he said.

"Is that what made you decide to become a world traveler?" Sonny asked.

"Well, that and being drunk—just once, mind you—while giving the sermon. That was what really made me decide to take to the rails. I guess it really wasn't my idea as much as it was the church elders," he said, smiling.

"Is that fellow on the porch really your brother?" Charlie asked.

"We are all brothers in the eyes of God. But if you mean my actual dyed-in-the-wool share-the-same-bloodline brother, then no," he said. "Clarence is another lost soul, I guess. Can you boys tell he is of the Mexican line of folks, unlike me who is from the African bloodline? We call him Clarence but his real name is Manuel. I would tell you his last name but in the world we exist in, we don't use last names.I know Manuel is from somewhere down in South Texas. He was the caretaker of a large cemetery but he got canned or run off, however you want to look at it, I suppose. I was talking with him on a train from Dallas to Oklahoma City about his job but getting any information out of him is about as easy as peeing on a fence. Once he found out I was an ex-preacher, he started to open up somewhat. Manuel took to the cemetery with such gusto that it wasn't any time until he knew the names of each person buried there. He even knew the date most of them were born and died. After years working in the cemetery, he started to think of those in the graves as his family. Apparently, over the years working, Manuel would overhear several of the people that came to the cemetery to visit with their departed loved ones. He said the people who came out to visit would tell their departed such things as how their children were doing, like if they are being good or bad. Most were bad things like, 'Little Sally tied her cat's tail to the clothesline' or 'Little Sally got pregnant by the boy down the street' or how their family was going broke, they didn't know if they had enough money to even eat on. All the bad things family members were telling his graveyard family started to weigh on Manuel. Several times when he would overhear someone telling one of the dearly departed something negative, he would run over and say something like, 'Don't you know, Mr. and Mrs. Dearborn don't give a crap if your husband is messing around on you' or 'This person is at rest, why don't you take you negative butt out of here!' He would scream at them. Seemed every time he would confront a family member about what they were saying to one of his underground family, they would report him for speaking up. Several times, he got his pay docked or sent home for a few days without pay.

"One afternoon, he was talking to a gypsy family who stopped by, selling cures for just about everything that had a name. If it had a name, they had a cure for it. The head gypsy told Manuel that family members shouldn't tell their dearly departed negative things because a soul could not go to his reward with negative thoughts in their hearts. Because once a person walks through those pearly gates, all they can experience then are love and happiness. He figured there must be just a whole bunch of benches around the pearly gates where souls that have negative thought have to sit around and wait until those thoughts were completely out of their minds and hearts. Said it wouldn't surprise him one little bit if some of them have been sitting on those benches for years. Take Noah, for instance. People have been talking about him from day one so old Noah sits on a bench watching people walk in all day long. So, Manuel decides to fix that problem once and for all. One evening after the gates were closed, he took the truck and started knocking all the headstones over. Then he loaded the stones into the back of the truck. Each time the truck was full of headstones, he would head to the river bridge and toss

R. J. Burroughs

those stones in. Then he'd head back for the next load. I am
told it took around ten to fifteen loads to get the job done,"
Jordan said to the boys, wiping the sweat off his forehead.

"Gosh almighty, why would he do something like that?
Did he go nuts from working all that time at the graveyard?"
Gary asked.

"Apparently, Manuel got the idea that if the family
members couldn't find the grave of their loved ones, then
they couldn't tell them about the problems going on in their
daily lives. That's why he took the headstones. He figured
all his underground family could now get off the benches
they were setting on, go on into heaven, and experience the
love and happiness," he continued.

"I bet the family members finding all the headstones
gone didn't take to that real kindly," Charlie answered.

"That's a pure fact. The cops arrested him the very next
day. When he went up in front of the judge and told him
the story about the benches and his underground family, the
judge dropped the charges. Bu, he did send Manuel to the
booby hatch for observation. Manuel ended up spending
nine months in the booby hatch before they decided he
was fit to live with normal folk. But to this very day, all
he talks about is getting back to the graveyard to see his
underground family," Jordan said.

The boys hung around with Billy and the others for
a couple of more hours. Lillie May made the boys some

sandwiches to eat on their walk back, Billy told Charlie to tell his brother to stop his worrying about him. After all, he was a full-grown man.

15

That evening when the boys got back from Billy's house, there wasn't much to do. There was a movie showing but the boys thought it had to be a girly movie from the posters. Besides, they wanted to save what little money they had for the movie, *The Time Machine*, which was showing on Saturday. Gary suggested playing Flower on the Tombstone. The other boys tried to act as if they liked playing that game but the truth was that none of them really cared for it. They were too chicken to tell the others. They all headed to the graveyard, stopping by Jake's house on the way to pick up a baseball.

"Who goes first? If I remember correctly, it was Jake that was next up for the baseball," Gary said.

"Okay, I'll start it off," Jake said.

Flower on the Tombstone is a game played after dark. One boy would walk into the cemetery with a flower, find a tombstone someplace in the graveyard, then place the flower on top of it. Then it was up to the other boys to go in and find the flower, one at a time. But the boys thought a flower was too girly, so they chose a baseball in its place. While a person was hunting the ball, if one or two of the other guys wanted to go in and try to scare that person... well, that just made the game all that more exciting.

As the other boys stood by the gate to the cemetery, Jake took the baseball and started in. Just before he was completely out of sight from the others, he turned around and looked at the other guys standing around and watching him. Jake had the look of someone that just had his Halloween candy taken by a couple of older boys, or a fellow that was just about to walk up the thirteen steps to the gallows. Sonny and Charlie started to go inside to hide behind something and scare Jake as he was walking back out. But remembering the look Jake had on his face walking in, they just didn't have the heart to do it. Inside the graveyard, Jake felt like his life as he knew it was now going to be over. If there were really such things as ghosts milling around the place and he happened to bump into one of them, he figured he would have a heart attack, plain and simple. It was just as easy as that. Maybe one would be hiding behind a headstone just waiting to float up in front of him as he walked up.

Bumping into a headstone that was only knee-high, Jake let out a little yelp. "Whoever thinks it is cool to put up only half a headstone should be given a heck of a talking to. Or better yet, just outright killed for putting up only half a tombstone. I bet the deceased wouldn't like it either. If they only knew," he whispered to himself as he rubbed his leg.

Standing there rubbing his leg, Jake wondered if a ghost did happen to appear to him, would he wet his pants before he died from a heart attack? He said a little prayer that if he died tonight, that he only had to pee in his pants from being so scared, instead of going number two. If he did the other and they got the ambulance to save his life, he would never get over it. Jake knew that if he put the baseball on one of the headstones only a little ways from the entrance gate, the guys would tease him about being a scared little girl who was afraid to go deep into the cemetery. With that thought, he decided to walk over the hill and put the baseball on one of the headstones in the lower part of the cemetery. As he topped the hill, the sight of a light surprised him. Afraid that someone might see him, he ducked down behind a tombstone. He read the inscription, "Charles and Rosa Darragh." They both died in the 40's.

Still scared half to death, he sat behind the Charles-and-Rosa tombstone, watching the two men in the light. It looked to him as if they were digging something up. Jake placed the baseball on Charles and Rosa's tombstone then he crawled back toward the gate. Once he was over the top of the hill, he stood back up and quickly made his way to the gate and his friends.

Jake said, "Guys, there are a couple of men in there. They are just over the hill, out of sight of anyone who might come around."

"I bet it's a couple of high school guys or a couple of guys doing a little drinking and don't want to be seen by anyone," Bruce said.

"Well, if its high school guys or drinkers, wonder why they are digging?" Jake asked, looking at the others in the dark and trying to see the expressions on their faces.

"You say they are digging? Digging in the graveyard?" Gary asked.

"Yes, I was up close enough to see what they were doing and they were digging. I wasn't able to hear what they were saying. I guess I could have tried to get closer but I figured I better come back let you guys know what was going on," Jake said.

"Well, if they are digging, you know what that means, don't you?" he asked.

"Excuse me, but do you think you might tell us what it means?" Jake asked.

"Fellows, it means we have stumbled upon grave robbers. You can just about bet they're not there digging up worms for a fishing trip inside a graveyard," Sonny said.

"Grave robbers! What in the world would grave robbers be doing in Verden?" Charlie said.

"Robbing graves isn't that what grave robbers do?" Jake answered.

"Think we should go call the sheriff or tell someone?" Charlie asked no one in particular.

"What if we call the sheriff then he comes out here to arrest the grave robbers and they are just a couple of guys drinking? That Jake made a mistake and they are not digging at all? Then you can just about bet he will be mad as all get-out," Sonny said.

"Well, then we have to go in and see if they are robbing graves or drinking or whatever it is before we tell anyone," Jake suggested.

Deciding to check it out, the boys all went into the graveyard. Once they were close to the top of the little hill, they got down on all fours and crawled from gravestone to gravestone, trying not to be seen. Jake was beside Sonny when they got close enough to see the two men. The boys figured it was a Coleman lantern sitting on a nearby tombstone that was giving off light. One fellow was also holding a flashlight to light up the area for the other man who was digging. All the boys stayed behind the markers because every once in a while, the guy with the flashlight would shine it around the area to see if anyone might be on to them or coming toward them.

"Jake was right. They have to be grave robbers. There ain't no other reason a person would be digging in the dark of night in a city graveyard," Sonny whispered to Charlie.

"What you think they are after?" Charlie replied.

"Well, like I said before, two men digging in a graveyard at night and you can just about bet they are up to no good," Sonny answered.

"That don't tell me nothing. Heck, we are up to no good being here ourselves."

"I bet they are not just grave robbers, they are also treasure hunters."

"Treasure hunters? There isn't any treasure in the middle of a graveyard," Charlie said.

"No, really, there are treasures here. When someone's family member dies, people have a habit of leaving expensive jewelry on them, rings, necklaces, and such. I once heard of a movie star that died and when they buried her, she was wearing a ten-thousand-dollar ring and a necklace that was worth up to a hundred thousand dollars," Sonny whispered back to Charlie.

"I wonder why folks do that. Isn't like anyone will ever see the stuff again," Gary said.

"Movie stars do it all the time," Sonny insisted.

"Well, as far as I know, there isn't any movie stares buried anywhere around here," Charlie countered. "Unless you count Neil Popper. Wasn't he in a cowboy movie once?"

"Yes, he was. But he only played a dead body. No one ever got to see his face so you really can't count him," Sonny answered.

The boys were lucky that the breeze was blowing the leaves in the trees, muffling the sound of their voices as they whispered to one another. It was just enough to keep the sounds away from the two men. However, the direction of the breeze carried the voices of the gravediggers to the boys.

"I've hit something," the man who was down in the grave said up to the man leaning over him.

"What you think it is?" the man at the top answered.

"'What do you think it is?' Did that guy really say that? What could it be?" Charlie asked. "Let's see, he is digging in a graveyard, hits something in the grave, and wonders what it is. What the heck could it be other than a coffin?" Charlie snickered.

"Tie this rope around the bottom so we can pull it up," the man said, tossing down a rope.

Once they were both on top, the guy who had been the grave digger said, "Not sure about this. It's awfully old. Not sure if the handle I tied to will hold or not."

"Okay, as we pull, try not to jerk the rope. Pull in nice smooth pulls," the other guy answered.

The boys, watching from behind different markers, wondered if these two men would be able to pull the casket out of the grave. After watching for several minutes in the dim light, a casket began to emerge. First, the back appeared. Then more and more of the coffin became visible until the two men had it completely out of the ground and resting next to the hole.

"Here, take this and pry it open," the digger said to the other.

"Me? How in the hell did you come up with the idea I should open it?" the other guy complained.

"Give it back to me then," the digger snapped.

The boys could hear the scratching sound as the man tried to insert the screwdriver into the lid of the coffin. He worked for several minutes before a popping sound was heard. Both men were leaning over the casket as the digger raised the lid. The smell coming from the coffin hit both men at the same time, and it knocked both of them off their feet.

"Good Lord Almighty, what the heck?" came from one of the fellows.

The smell was so bad the boys caught a whiff of the overpowering odor in the light breeze coming toward them. Charlie pulled up his shirt to cover his face. Sonny grabbed a handful of flowers that was on top of the marker he was hiding behind. Finding they were artificial, he tossed them aside and pulled his shirt up as well.

The two men got back up, slowly, very slowly. They approached the casket again. The man with the flashlight aimed the beam inside the coffin, and seeing whatever he saw, he said, "Crap! That isn't Mildred. Who is that?" He turned to the other fellow. "You idiot! You dug on the wrong side of the marker. Mildred Rankin is on the other side."

"Well, let's just dig on that side," answered the other fellow.

"There is no way in hell we are going to push our luck and spend another three hours out here. Just pick up your stuff and let's get out of here," the man with the flashlight said.

Sonny and Charlie watched the two men put the lantern light out, tossed a few things in a bag, then head out of the cemetery, taking the other direction from the way the boys came in. When the boys were sure they were gone and figured—or hoped—they wouldn't be coming back, they all met by the tombstone Charlie and Sonny were hiding behind.

"What now?" Gary asked.

"Well, I guess some of us need to wait here while the others go tell someone what happened," Charlie said.

"Well, you can just about bet the farm I'm not going to be one of the ones that stay here," Jake said.

"If Charlie will stay with me, I'll wait here until you guys get back," Sonny volunteered.

"I will stay but I want to let everyone know right off the bat that it's under protest," Charlie grumbled.

"Under protest? What are you talking about *under protest*?" Bruce asked.

"I'll tell you why. First, I am not sure if we are even supposed to be in here after dark. Second, we have been watching two fellows robbing a grave. Third, we have no clue if they will show up again. And lastly, it just isn't normal to be sitting just a few feet away from a dead body that has been at rest for God knows how long," Charlie elaborated. "Also, I don't know a lot about ghosts, goblins, zombies, devils and such, but if there ever was a chance to run into one of them dudes…well, this would be a perfect place to do it. We have no idea who they dug up and left in that coffin over there," Charlie said with a noticeable fear in his voice.

"Okay, then. Jake, Bruce, and I will run to town and call the law or have someone call them for us, while Sonny and Charlie wait and watch here," Bruce said.

With that said, the three boys turned and headed off into the night, leaving Charlie and Sonny leaning up against a grave marker.

"You know, over the years, we have done some really stupid stuff but I believe hands down this has to be right there at the top of stupid things we have gotten into," Charlie whispered to Sonny.

"Why is that, Charlie?" Sonny asked.

"Like I said before, we have no clue who is in that casket. If it's some Christian man or woman who died naturally by a heart attack or growing old, well, that would be fine I guess. But, if it's someone who has been murdered or died in a car wreck—something I like to call a surprise death— then that could be kind of a bad deal for you and me."

"What do you mean by *surprise death*? Aren't all deaths a surprise?"

"Of course not. Take Old Man Bruner. Remember him? He is that old fellow who passed away last year from just being old. Well, all his family was with him when he went on to the kingdom. They all knew he was going to die. That's why they all gathered around him when he left. Now that is a normal passing away. No surprise at all. He just up and died with everyone telling him bye."

"I have no clue what you are talking about, Charlie," Sonny said, trying to smile at his buddy.

"Okay, then, take Lena Lawson. If you remember, she was heading to her mother's house for something or other. If I remember correctly, she was out of bread and walked to her mother's house to borrow a loaf. On the way back, she was crossing Highway 62 and got herself run smooth over by some Indian fellow. There she lay dead on the highway with pieces of rainbow bread scattered everywhere around her."

"So?"

"Sonny, you sure need to try to keep up with this story. When she was hit and killed by the Indian fellow, *that* was a surprise death because she had no clue she was fixing to die. I figure her plan was to get that bread, go home, and have pinto beans, fried potatoes, and that bread. Instead, she got run over and killed."

"Again, Charlie, so what?"

"Sonny, it is a proven fact that when a person has a surprise death, they have to hang around here on earth for the same number of years they would have lived iffin' they hadn't been killed untimely," Charlie continued with his explanation. "I figure the Lord didn't have a plan for that Indian fellow to run over Lena so it would mess up his plan to be bringing her up there with him until it was her time.

If he did, it might just cause a backup of folks fixing to get in up there in heaven."

"So you're telling me that Lena Lawson is hanging around in this world doing nothing until she has been here the same number of years she would have lived if she hadn't been killed by the Indian fellow?" Sonny asked.

"Now you're getting it. Except, Lena isn't just hanging around down here doing nothing. I figure if she was, say, thirty when she got herself killed and was suppose to be here until she died at, say, eighty-five…well, that leaves fifty-five years to hang around doing nothing because there isn't much a ghost can do, being dead and all. So I figure she haunts folks just to have something to do," Charlie said. "Now do you get my point? Whoever is lying over there in that casket, if they died by surprise, then they could very well be right here madder than all get-out about those two fellows were digging their body up. And since the two fellows are long gone, that just leaves you and me for him or her to vent their anger on." Charlie started looking around in the darkness.

Sonny really didn't have an answer for that other than looking around into the darkness as well, hoping not to see anything. "What if we go over there and tell whoever it is in the casket that we are sorry they got themselves dug up? That we are only here as a favor to them? Think that would make them feel any better?" Sonny asked Charlie.

"It might, and it might not. I'm no authority on crap like this," Charlie said.

"Well, you seemed to know a lot about it when you were telling me about surprise death and normal death."

"Well, it might help to go over there and explain ourselves."

"Go over there and explain to a dead guy or girl who has been dead for a long time? What do we do? Just peek into the casket and talk? I think not," Sonny answered. "If it's all the same to you, I think I would just like to wait until the others get back."

"Sure, that makes perfect sense to me," Charlie agreed.

About the same time Charlie said that, a large bird took off flying only a couple feet above the boys' heads.

"What the hell was that? A hoot owl or what?" Charlie asked.

"Search me. If it was an owl, then what made it fly away? We weren't making any noise to frighten the thing," Sonny replied.

"Well, there you go. Something had to scare the darn thing, and if it wasn't you or me, then what could it have been?" Charlie peered into the darkness, still hoping not to see anything. His voice shaking, Charlie asked Sonny, "You have any matches?"

"Yes, I got a book that has about half the matches left in it," Sonny answered.

"Well, then, we have two choices. We can run like a couple of kindergarten kids out of here or we can crawl over there and tell whoever is in that box we are here only to help them."

"I have no problem running out of here like a couple of kids."

"That sounds like a good choice to me but the only thing is, what if it were to come after us? I sure don't want no ghost messing around with me for who knows how long."

"Seems like I read someplace if a ghost has its eye on a person, it keeps after that person until they go plumb nuts. Or until it's time for the ghost to head on up or down to its rewards, whichever direction their reward happens to be taking them."

"So, what are you trying to say?" Sonny asked.

"Well, I sure hate to say it, but it looks as if one of us has to go over there and talk to whoever is in that casket if we want to live a normal life," Charlie answered.

"One of us? Which *one of us* did you have in mind to do that?" Sonny asked. "Well, you can just about bet I'm not going over there by myself. And that, my friend, is a pure fact."

"Okay, let's both go. That way, maybe it—whatever it is—might not do anything."

"Do anything? Do what? What the heck you talking about *do anything*?"

"I don't know. I guess do whatever it is mad ghosts do?"

"Okay, then let's do this."

The two boys crawled from behind the tombstone. One crawled around one side, while the other crawled out the other side. The boys could have stood up and walked up to the coffin but their minds were on whoever might be in it and what they might see when they got to it. Most of all, they wondered if all the things Charlie had been talking about might have just a smidgen of truth in it. So they just forgot to get up on their feet. Once they reached the coffin, they couldn't see anything inside of it from the darkness.

"Good Lord, this stink will kill a fellow. Smells like something died around here," Charlie said, looking at Sonny in the darkness.

Sonny had to smile at hearing those words from Charlie. Grinning, he looked into Charlie's face in the darkness, tipped his head toward the coffin, and said, "Duh!"

"Well, you going to strike one of those matches so we can see in or not?"

Charlie asked.

Sonny pulled the book of matches out of his back pocket, broke one off, and struck it. When it lit, the boys both got a glimpse into the casket and they fell back as if they had just seen a ghost.

"Good gosh! They dug up Wanda Clayton," Sonny exclaimed.

"Yes, I saw that just the same as you did," Charlie said. "Was that a dog lying beside her?"

"Yes, Wanda never went any place without her dog. Bullet, I believe was its name."

"I only know this and that about her, things I overheard my folks talking about after she was killed."

"I know all about her. My grandmother was a friend of hers—if you can believe my grandmother was ever friendly with anyone by the way she talks to us. But she was, and she talked about her a lot," Sonny whispered to Charlie, as both boys scooted on their butts back a few feet from the casket. "She died when we were around six years old."

"So she has been buried for about eight years then," Charlie stated.

"Wow, that's right! I guess you didn't sleep through all your math classes," Sonny said to Charlie, trying to hit him on his shoulder so Charlie would understand he was just kidding with him. "My grandmother said Wanda Clayton was her name but back before she was put in that thing, everyone around Verden called her Wandering Wanda. My granny told me she never went anywhere without her dog.

All she ever did was wander around town, never going anywhere in particular, just her and her dog. Woman never went anywhere without her dog." Sonny asked, "You know that house east of town? The big white one? The one with the big pillars out in front?"

"Sure, I have been by there several times with my folks," Charlie answered "Well, that was her house. Wanda had more money than the law allowed. My grandmother said not once did she ever cash a social security check. People from town believed she kept her money someplace in her house, like in a mattress or a wall safe, because she didn't trust banks. Course, I guess that isn't completely true. According to my grandmother, it isn't banks she didn't trust, it was the people that worked at the bank she didn't trust. The way I heard it, she was married to a big shot banker in Oklahoma City, came home one evening and caught him—"

"She found him with another woman, I bet," Charlie interrupted.

"You know, that's the same thing I said before my grandmother could finish talking, just like you just did to me," Sonny answered. "But the truth is a lot stranger than that. She found her husband in the bathroom just as naked as the day his mom popped him out into the new world. He was naked and lying in the bathtub half-filled of water with money all around him, floating above and in the water."

"Bullcrap! That can't be true. Who would do something like that?" Charlie asked.

"I tell you, it's a God-given fact. She walked in that bathroom expecting to see her hubby taking a hot bath from a hard day's work, but finding him washing his old naked self with dollar bills, twenties, and—I suspect—even some of them hundreds as well," Sonny said, grinning from ear to ear.

"Now why would a man do something like that? It doesn't make any sense. Besides, he was a banker. He worked with money all day long."

"You know, Charlie, I don't think you get out nearly enough, and that, my boy, is a fact. Have you ever even been in a library?"

"I never had any need to go into the library because I have you. And you seem to know a little about everything so all I have to do is ask you." Charlie laughed out loud but he caught himself, thinking it might not be proper to laugh that loud in a graveyard.

"People do all kinds of strange things in the world. I read about a woman who prayed twelve hours a day, asking that her dog be turned into a man so she would have someone to marry." Sonny said.

"He ever turned? Because if he did, I know a cute little cat that might make a great girlfriend," Charlie joked.

"And take my grandmother, she won't go to bed or sit down at the breakfast table without first looking under it. I guess her brother Charles had a habit of hiding under her bed and he would scare the holy water out of her. So to this day, she still looks under her bed. Charles stopped scaring her twenty something years ago after he had that heart attack and died. Anyway, finding her husband in that bathtub that way, she up and divorced him right on the spot. She was afraid if he would take a bath with money, then there sure wasn't any way she could sleep beside him. No telling what his sick perverted mind might decide to do during the night.

After the divorce, Wanda and her two boys moved here to Verden. She bought that house with the pillars. Her boys went to Verden schools as well. During the war, she got two telegrams just two days apart, telling her that her first son, Leroy, was killed on Saipan and her other son was killed on a Utah beach.

After her boys were killed, she just kind of lost her mind and started wandering around Verden day and night. Never talked to anyone she passed but she would go to my grandmother now and then. My grandmother said she even seen her and her dog in Chickasha one afternoon just walking around," Sonny said.

"Well, what happened to her? How did she end up here?" Charlie asked.

"She was walking down Main Street one morning, an hour or two before daylight, and some farmer ran over her with his John Deer tractor. Killed her and her dog, just like that. They was both on their way to the promised land before either one of them hit the ground. Course, I'm not sure if dogs go there or not, but she did, and in her will, she asked to be buried with her dog at her side." Sonny looked around hoping to see a light from his friends coming back with the law.

"I think your blowing smoke up my butt, my friend. I have never heard of any dogs getting embalmed," Charlie declared.

"If you had paid more attention when you looked in at her, you would have seen she still looks pretty good but the dog has rotted away. That's why it stinks when they opened the casket," Sonny continued.

"Guys, guys," Sonny and Charlie heard the others coming their way.

When Jake and the others found them, they had the town police officer along with the sheriff himself. The police officer gave the boys a ride home, telling them to stay out of the cemetery after dark from then on. The grave robbers were never found.

The story went around town. It didn't take but a couple of days when people were telling one another that there were ten or more grave robbers. And when the boys walked up on them, lots of shots were fired at the boys. The boys thought they would be big men around town and considered as heroes after what happened at the cemetery. However, it didn't work out as they thought it would.

Jake's parents made him start coming in by nine o'clock. It felt as bad as being made to come in by noon since it was the last few days until summer would be over. Gary got grounded until school started for telling his mother he was going to a Sunday school function, knowing all the while that he and his buddies were going to the graveyard. Bruce's parents were really mad and he was grounded indefinitely. Charlie's folks just gave him a few extra chores to do around the house. That wouldn't have been too bad, except they told him he had to do the extra chores until the next school season was at least half over.

Sonny's mother and grandmother sat him down at the table and gave him a talking-to, which was something he hated.

His grandmother ended with, "Boy, if you dare do something like that again, I will set my alarm clock to wake me up around four in the morning. By 4:15 a.m., I will be whooping your butt with my flyswatter until noon. Then after lunch, I will start whipping your butt again until supper. A boy of fourteen should have enough sense to know that no good could ever come from being in a graveyard after dark."

Sonny could have told her he had no plans whatsoever in going to the cemetery again after dark but this was due to the talk he and Charlie had while waiting for the other boys to get back with help.

16

The boys decided to try to have another adventure before they had to get back into the grind of school. At least, three of them did. Gary and Bruce were still grounded. Bruce didn't bother to try to talk his way out of it, but Gary tried his best to convince his parents to lift his punishment. However, there was no give at all from his parents.

"The way they are treating me, I will be lucky to get out of the house after I get married," Gary told the boys.

"After you get married? Don't worry about that, no girl would have you," Sonny teased.

Jake was finely able to talk his mother into letting him go with the other boys. After several hours of begging, she finely broke down and let him go after he promised he wouldn't get into any more trouble. The other boys knew that keeping that promise would be about as easy as a fart staying together in an Oklahoma windstorm.

The boys decided to go to a place called Peck's Landing, a place at a small little bend in the river about halfway between Verden and Anadarko. It would be a long walk but it was something to do at least. The day after the boys had the run-in with the grave robbers, Sonny and Jake were sitting on the porch and talking to Jake's older brother. They were telling him about all that happened to them at the graveyard the night before.

"Well, have you boys ever heard of a place called Peck's Landing?" he asked them.

Neither boy had any idea what Peck's Landing was but you can bet that as soon as they heard of it, you couldn't pull the boy's attention away from Joe with a bulldozer. Jake's brother, Joe, was six years older than Jake. It wasn't often Joe that would have anything to do with Jake, thinking him too young to mess with. However, that didn't seem to be the case that day as he sat on the porch with the two boys, talking to them as if he was a member of their bunch.

"Well, guys, about four—or it could have been five years ago, I'm not real sure—there was a family who lived along the bend of the river at the very end of North-South Road 344. The Pecks or the Pecks family was what a fellow would call a hermit family. When the family needed something, only the father and eldest son would come to town to get whatever it was they needed. They would never talk to anyone other than the person they were doing business with," Joe said, starting to tell them the story. "I happened to be at the store one afternoon, getting myself a moon pie and a Coke when the Pecks came in to pick up a few things, like potatoes and such. Some fellow walked up to Mr. Peck and asked, 'How you boys doing? Isn't it a fine day?' The fellow must have not known the reputation of the Pecks because he was just visiting in town or something, but he found out right quick. Mr. Peck turned to him and said, 'Fellow, I got me no clue who you are. As for the weather, it is a nice day for a butt whooping so I suggest you go about whatever it was that brought you in here and leave us purely alone.' That old boy had no clue how to take the Pecks so he just ups and pays for his bologna and cheese and walks out of the place, shaking his head in disbelief. The Pecks went on about their business, packed up their things, and left without another word."

"Were you close enough to see the guy buying baloney and cheese?"

Jake asked his brother.

"No, I was at the back of the store but I figured the guy was heading to Lake Chickasha. And everyone knows that when people go to the lake for the day, they always have baloney and cheese with them," Joe answered. Both boys nodded their heads in agreement about the baloney and cheese as if it was a known fact.

"Was Mr. Peck an old man?" Jake asked.

"I'm not good at telling someone's age, but I figure he was about forty-five or fifty when I last saw him," Joe said. "He wasn't a real big man but he always wore bib overalls with an old black felt hat. He also had a full white beard.

And he always looked like he was mad at someone or mad at the world, I guess I should say." Jake sat down on the edge of the porch closer to the two boys. "The Pecks had two daughters but the only chance a person ever had to see the girls was if they happened to be in the front yard or tending the garden when they drove by the house. Mr. Peck wouldn't allow those girls to go to school, church, or any place they might encounter people other than family. I believe that was because he didn't trust women at all. You see, Mrs. Peck took off for a weekend once with a fellow who sold manure and eggs to the folks around the area. The Pecks have had their own chickens but I guess they were short on manure most times. Anyways, the manure man spent a lot of time out at the Peck's, so one weekend, Mrs. Peck just up and left with him for the whole weekend. The manure man had her thinking he was rich from all the manure he had sold over the years. But she come to find out he wasn't just selling manure, he was full of manure as well because after the weekend, he just up and left Mrs. Peck in the motel in Chickasha. So having no alternative, Mrs. Peck had to go back home and beg her husband for forgiveness."

"Did he take her back?" Sonny asked.

"Fact is, he did. But you know what, fellows? She came up missing no more than a week after she went back home. Most folks around town figured Mr. Peck done her in for her being an adulteress. Cops even went out there and talked to him but there being no body, they couldn't get him for nothing. Can't arrest a fellow for just being a butthole now, can you?" Joe asked, looking to each of the two boys. "Then over the next four years, all his family came up missing. Most folks figured he done them in one by one as well. After his wife did what she did, he just flipped out and became one of them serial killers. But there were still no bodies So there was nothing they could do to him.

People around town were sure he was doing his family in, but like I said, there was no body. They tried to send him to the nuthouse but the judge wouldn't allow that either. Then one day, the sheriff when out there to ask him a couple more questions, and—this is a fact, fellows—he was nowhere to be found. When they went into the house, everything was just as if everyone was still living there. Girls' things were hanging in the closet, the boys as well. Just no one around. Cops even had a couple of men camp out right there for a month, watching the place but nothing ever happened, nor did any of the family ever come back to claim anything. So making a long story shorter, people from town believe Mr. Peck is still out there, watching his house and watching over the graves of his family members he did in. People have hunted and hunted for graves but as of today, no one has found anything yet. However, strange things seem to happen around what is now called Peck's Landing. People who park their cars there to go fishing, seem to always get something or other stolen. Or they get the side of their cars scratched by someone. One fellow even got the words *Leave here* scratched in his car in two different places."

As soon as Joe finished telling them about the Pecks, the boys headed right over to Charlie's house and talked his folks into letting him join them for one last time. His mother went ahead and let him go since school would be starting so soon. The three boys decided to take their camping stuff to make the long walk to Peck's Landing, check things out when they got there, then spend the night. They planned to make their way back home the next afternoon. After gathering up everything the boys figured they might need for their night out, they set out for Peck's Landing. As they walked along, things didn't feel the same with their other friends not being able to come along.

"How will we be able to recognize a grave if we happen to stumble upon one?" Jake asked Sonny.

"Search me. I guess if we happen to see a spot that might just look a little different than the ground around it or if it's a grave, it might be sunken in somewhat. Other than that, I guess we just play it by ear," Sonny answered.

It took the boys about an hour and half to make the four-mile walk. On the way, they talked just about everything they could think of, including school starting again and Mary Sue Bailey. Mary Sue was the girl Sonny had his eye on since he became aware girls were different than boys.

"You know, Sonny, if I was you, I don't think I would unsnap any girl's bra this year," Jake teased.

"Well, there is no need for you to worry yourself over that. I have no plans to do anything like that ever again. Believe me, that one time was enough for me. If I ever get married and my wife asked me to unsnap her bra for her, I would have to think twice before I even considered doing it," Sonny assured his friends.

"Okay, here's the deal. I wasn't there when Jake's brother told you about this Peck's place. But if they never found him or any of the family, how do we know they are not still somewhere around the place?" Charlie asked.

"Well, if they were there after all these years, you can just about bet someone or other would have seen them by now," Jake reasoned.

Walking down the dirt road, they were almost right in front of the Pecks' house before they knew it. The roadside had been covered by brush and blackjack trees then it stopped abruptly, and they saw the house. It was set back maybe fifty yards from the road. The house had been painted white but most of the paint had long ago been weather-beaten and faded from the wood. The house didn't look much different than several of the homes in Verden. The difference was that this house had a history. A house is just a house, but when a house has a history of evil—or what people perceive as evil—surrounding it, that changes the way people look at it.

"Let's go look through the windows," Charlie said.

Jake and Sonny were hesitant, being the only two that heard Joe tell the story of Mr. Peck. But hesitant or not, the two went with Charlie to look in the windows. They did it because to fourteen-year-old boys, saving face is about the most important thing in their lives. Looking in the front picture window, it seemed as if the family had just left for vacation. The furniture was covered with sheets to protect it from dust or mice or anything that might harm them.

The bend in the river was about two or three hundred yards from the house. The boys headed on down toward it. Finding a clear spot about fifteen feet from the water, they set up their tent. Then they went looking for anything that might not look like it belonged there. The three boys looked for a couple of hours until the sun was about to set. Sitting outside their tent, the boys ate beanie weenies and some cold chicken Jake's mother fixed for their overnight trip. Sipping warm RC Cola, the boys were discussing what each one of them thought about Peck's Landing, Mr. Peck, and his family.

"I bet his wife probably just up and got a gutful of Mr. Peck then took off to unknown places," Jake said. "And it wouldn't surprise me one bit if his kids got a gutful of him as well and went off to live with aunts and uncles or just friends. If you remember, Joe said this Peck fellow was a mean old through and through."

The boys sat and talked about the missing family until it was completely dark. The boys didn't notice the darkness because of the bright moon that evening. Once they realized it was completely dark, the boys talked about what they thought might have happened to the family. It seemed okay to them to talk about such things in the light of day but it was dark now and they were unable to see what was going on out in the woods. Realizing that what might have happened to the Peck family occurred only a short ways from their tent, none of the boys wanted to admit that each one of them was scared. About 11:45 p.m., the boys finally drifted off to sleep.

Charlie thought he heard something or other outside. He didn't know for sure what it was or if he heard anything at all. He knew he was prone to dreaming, so he checked his watch and saw that it was 12:30. Deciding he must have heard a raccoon, skunk, or some other critter prowling around outside looking for food, he laid his head back on the backpack he was using as a pillow. After a couple of minutes or so, he was just about to fall back to sleep when he heard something again. This time, he knew he wasn't dreaming. He sat back up and moved between the two other boys to look outside. There was nothing anywhere around that he could see so he again figured it was some kind of a critter moving around in the bushes. He was about ready to scream out from the tent in hopes of scaring whatever it was that was lurking around their tent. Sticking his head out a little, he noticed a man up on the ledge several feet away from him. The man was looking down on their campsite and directly on him.

As he looked at the figure, his eyes adjusted a bit better to the dim moonlight. What he saw scared him so bad that he couldn't get a scream out of his mouth. It was a well-deserved scream because what he saw appeared to be an older man wearing a hat of some kind. It wasn't a baseball cap like most guys around town wore, but it looked like a full felt hat to him. He saw that the man also had a full beard. The figure then turned and walked down the other side of the rise. When it was completely out of Charlie's sight, all the nerve he lost when he first saw the figure started to return to him. It didn't come back in one big wave like it left him; it started coming back to him in spurts. First, he felt his legs under him; then the feeling started to return to his shoulders and arms. After a few seconds, Charlie was able to grunt a little, and then the sounds started to come back to his mouth.

"Guys! Guys!" he screamed loud enough to wake the dead.

Jake sat straight up, looking around as if he was expecting to be hit by a truck or something. The look on his face showed pure panic.

Sonny jumped up about the same as Jake, except he put out a few words with his panicked look. "Good God, you near scared me to death! What the hell were you thinking, screaming out like that?"

"I just saw an old guy standing on that hill looking down at us," he said, still pretty much shaken.

"I believe all you saw was your imagination playing tricks on you because I don't see anything up there now." Sonny snickered.

"I'm not fooling around! I did see an old guy up on that rise. I promise, I did. He was standing right up there." Charlie pointed to a spot on the small hill. "He had a banker's type hat on. It looked felt but I can't be sure in only the moonlight. He had a full beard as well."

"We told you what this Peck fellow looked like. So you are either trying to scare the crap out of us—something you are doing pretty darn good at—or your mind is playing tricks on you. If you want my thoughts on the matter, I would say it's in your mind because over the fourteen years I've known you, your mind has never impressed me all that much." Jake was trying to make light of a scary situation.

"I'm telling you the truth. While you two braincases are thinking I am just blowing smoke up your butts, that Peck fellow is just over that hill yonder, trying to decide if he is going to bludgeon us guys to death or strangle us," Charlie said.

"You got anything else in you backpack to eat, Sonny? This being scared makes a fellow hungry." Jake laughed.

"I think I have some chips and maybe a couple pieces of fudge left," Sonny answered.

"Well, break it out. This being scared is hungry work on a fellow," Jake said, still laughing.

"Laugh all you want but I did see an older looking guy up there," Charlie insisted.

"Okay. Well, what was he wearing? We didn't tell you what Joe said he always wore and what he looked like. So speak up. What did this fellow look like?" Sonny demanded.

"Well, it was dark so I only saw him in the moonlight," Charlie admitted.

"Okay, here we go. Charlie is trying to back off on this fellow," Jake said, still giggling.

"Bullcrap! I'm not backing off. All I said was I couldn't see him real well, but I did see that he was wearing a set of worn bib overalls," Charlie whispered to the other two boys.

When he said *bib overalls*, both boys stopped laughing just as quickly as someone had flipped a switch.

Charlie could see the expressions on their faces turn from grins to something else. He was sure that he had hit a nerve when he said what he said. "I couldn't see his face that good either but this guy I'm sure had a full beard," Charlie added.

That was when the expressions on the other two boys turned to fear as they looked at one another. Jake pulled the flaps together on the tent and then tried to zipped them closed. He left only a few inches open so they could look out into the darkness. Just as he was ready to turn to the others, something caught his eye. It was someone walking up the hill toward the boys.

"Look!" Jake said to the other boys.

All three boys looked out the small opening. "Good Lord, that's him! That has to be him. It's Peck," Jake said.

The boys watched the man as more and more of his body came into view. He walked closer, and fear ran through the boys. Then a young girl walked up and stood beside the man who was looking down on them.

Sonny said, "Good grief! That has to be one of his daughters. It has to be."

Just as Sonny said that, the man on the hill and the girl raised their right arms and pointed down at the tent the three boys were hiding in. The boys did everything in their power to not scream. Jake did his best not to wet himself but a little escaped into his jeans before he was able to get his bladder under control.

"I knew I should not have come out here with you two. Now we are going to die and no one will ever know where our bodies are," Charlie cried.

"Crap! I hate to die without getting a kiss from Mary Sue," Sonny said.

"I'm not completely sure but I don't think this is the time to be thinking about your love life when we are only seconds away from being murdered," Jake snapped. "At least since we are together now, we will be together in the afterlife."

"If it's okay with you two, I would just as soon not talk about the afterlife just yet. I still have my two legs under me so before I take a trip to the afterlife, there is going to be a footrace first. So, guys, we aren't on our way to the afterlife just yet. In a second, I'm going to unzip this flap and then we have to run like or lives depend on it. To tell the truth, I guess they do. So let's run down to the river and swim or wade across. One of us has to make it. That way, he can tell the cops what happened and let someone know. You guys ready to run?" Sonny asked.

"Okay, let's do this!" Charlie yelled to the other two.

"Before we go, if I don't make it, will one of you tell my folks I love them? And tell Mary Sue the same thing for me?" Sonny added.

"If we live through this, Sonny, I guess you know you will never live this Mary Sue thing down, don't you?" Jake teased. He tried to smile but couldn't get his mouth to do it.

"Here we go!" Sonny screamed as he pulled the zipper down, exposing the opening.

All three boys tried to get out of the opening at the same time. Once out, they headed for the river, running and falling and running some more. The three of them hit the water at the same time. The river was only about waist deep but the boys were in such a hurry they didn't realize it. They began swimming across, away from the danger that must be coming down on them.

"Jake, I didn't know you could swim so well. Charlie, you and Sonny aren't that bad either, especially with your shoes and clothes on."

Hearing the voice from the bank with a big belly laugh and what sounded like giggling from a girl as well, the three boys turned around. Standing on the bank watching the boys, stood Jake's brother, Joe, along with Joe's longtime girlfriend, Kathy Young. The three boys stood in the river, looking back at Joe as he pulled off the fake beard along with the hat he had been wearing.

"Shit! Shit, Joe! You almost scared us to death. What the heck would you have told Mom if you gave us a heart attack? You butthole you!" Jake hissed.

"Just some payback, little brothers, for the many times you have jumped out behind doors to scare me and all the crap you have put me through in the last fourteen years," he said.

"And you, Kathy, how could you let him do this? We could have died," Sonny said accusingly.

Kathy didn't answer him. She just stood there and laughed at the three of them in the river.

As they walked out of the water, the three were smiling from ear to ear since they realized they weren't going to die or be making a trip to the afterlife that night.

"You know, guys, I am kind of ready for school to start on Monday. I need the rest," Jake declared.

"Yes, I will second that. Besides, I have something to tell one of the girls when she shows up Monday as well," Charlie said.

Sonny knew who Charlie meant by that but he was so glad to be alive, he really didn't care. Besides, he knew Charlie was only fooling with him—or at least, he hoped he was only fooling with him.

CPSIA information can be obtained
at www.ICGtesting.com
Printed in the USA
LVOW12s1205130716
495510LV00003B/5/P